Bound by Blood and Danger

Jaxon Storm

Contents

CHAPTER 1

"**W**ho said you could go anywhere!" my mother screams from the kitchen.

"I did!" I yell back. I don't need her permission. She can leave whenever and go wherever, so can I.

If she chooses to sleep at some sleezy guy's house four days out of the week, I'm allowed to see my friends. She has no power over me. I know she doesn't actually care. It's an excuse to try to control me.

I pull my grey denim jacket on over my plain black t-shirt and walk out my bedroom door, letting it slam behind me.

"Well, in this house you listen to me!" Her shriek voice carries up the stairway as I rush down them. "And I say you can't."

I roll my eyes at her, not caring if she notices as I round the corner at the bottom of the stairs. "I don't care what you say."

As soon as she spots me, she gives me her signature glare—the angry glare I never see her without—, and points her half-smoked cigarette at me. Ash falls to the floor, smoke rises and vanishes into the air. "Don't use that tone with me."

Walking towards the front door, I make a quick stop to stand in front of her; the kitchen counter between us.

She sucks in a deep, smoke-filled breath with the cigarette between her smudged lipstick lips, and blows the smoke in my direction.

I lean across the counter to get into her face as much as possible. As I do , from the corner of my eye, I spot her pack of cigarettes sat on the counter to my right, just out of my reach. "I'll use whatever tone I want with you."

"Dory," I hear my sister say in a sweet voice from behind me. "Where are you going?"

"None of your business," I reply, whipping around to face her. "And I told you to quit calling me that."

"Misty," Mum says, looking over my shoulder at her sitting on the lounge. "Up to your room, now."

While looking at Mum and giving quick glances to the pack of cigarettes, I hear hear her clamber off the couch. "Yes, mummy."

"And take all your crap up with you."

"Yes, mummy." The happiness in her voice turns my stomach. I will never understand how she can accept the way mum treats her. The way she treats us. How does she love her after everything she's done—or more like, hasn't done?

I listen to her scrambling up the stairs with her armful of toys, dropping one or two on the steps on her way up.

Mum looks back at me, her expression more sour than before. "You too."

"You can't order me around," I spit at her. "I'll go where I want."

"I'm the parent here. You listen to me. Now get upstairs."

"Some parent," I say with venom. "When's my birthday?" I can't keep away the grin that stretches my features, knowing I got her.

"The seventeenth of May," she answers proudly.

My smile widens. "Twenty-fourth of April."

She scoffs and scrunches her nose up at me, turning away, ending our conversation.

Too easy, as always.

I smile at my obvious victory and head towards the front door, snatching the pack of smokes off the counter without her seeing as I walk past.

Outside, the strong gusts of wind blows my jacket out behind me. It whirls around the loose strands of overgrown hair falling out from under my favourite grey beanie and whips them into my eyes. I do my best to tuck them under but they just end up falling out again.

The sun hides behind grey clouds, giving the chill in the wind more strength. It bites through my jacket. I tuck the cigarettes into the hand pocket and pull the unbuttoned front around me.

I find relief from the wind in my shitty car. When it roars to life, my music blasts throughout the small space without delay. The strong, pounding beat eases my mind.

As I drive, I do my best to push my mother's words out of my head, but they play on repeat like the most frustrating broken record.

By the time I pull up to the almost empty parking lot and turn off my beaten old car, I have to remind myself to drop my shoulders, and release the tension in my jaw. I allow myself to sit for a minute in the silence, to calm down and relax before I step out and walk down the narrow dirt path to the field.

I force a small smile as a mask but when I spot my small group of crazy people it easily becomes real.

I'm greeted with a chorus of wild greetings from my three friends as I approach the dirty wooden table on the edge of the field that we chose as our meeting place four years ago.

"Hey! Dorian!"

"'Bout time you showed!"

"Kept us waiting long enough, mate."

"Sorry, guys," I say. "Mum."

With my short explanation, I receive a long understanding sigh from each of them.

"Are you any closer to moving out, mate?" Axel asks, sat on the seat.

Even while sitting on the chair, he's taller than Jonah sitting slouched on top of the table. Although, in Jonah's defence, the table is on a slight hill with Axel on the upside. In Axel's defence, he's a six foot seventeen year old.

Axel has mentioned how much he hates his height being the topic of conversations. Every person he meets lets him know he's tall for his age. He says there's only one good thing to being tall: the girls attracted to his height.

We've tried to tell his multiple times, it's not just his height they're attracted to, that's just a bonus to them.

He has short, dark brown hair, with the sides shorter than the top, that matches his dark brown eyes. His natural tan skin draws more attention to his bright smile. The light patchy stubble makes him appear older than us. Girls practically lining up to talk to him in school proved him to be the better looking on in the group.

I give him a single fake laugh, mocking the idea of moving out any time soon. "No," I sigh, "I still need to save a lot more to be able to afford it. Even if I get out as soon as I can, it will probably still be two years from now."

"What? You're telling me that job you have at that tiny fruit and veg store doesn't pay a lot?" Jonah teases.

I shove him off the end of the table and take his spot. "Shut up."

All three of them burst into laughter and I can't keep from joining in.

"What about your sister?" Wyatt asks, lying on the table top beside me, staring up at the clouded sky.

"What about her?" I scoff.

"What would happen to her?" He lifts himself up to look me in the eye. "Would you take her with you?"

His light hazel eyes hold kindness, emphasised by his dark skin and soft features. He runs his hand over his short, tight-curled black hair; showing off the muscles in his arm.

I will never understand the enjoyment of playing sports. Running. Tackles. Sprained ankles. Heatstroke. Torn muscles. I can't think of anything worse—except living with my mother. However, Wyatt gives it more appeal with the muscles he has built over the years from playing every sport known to man.

His long, thin body allows every muscle to stand out. I'd be lying if I said I had never considered joining a sports team just so I could be as ripped as Wyatt, but I couldn't seem to find the motivation or interest.

Would I take her with me? I sigh. "I- uh- I don't-"

"So, that's a, no," says Jonah, pulling Wyatt's soccer ball out from under the table with his foot.

"Well- I- I mean-," I stammer trying to put together a sentence, "Mum has proven she doesn't care about us countless times, but Misty still loves her unconditionally."

"Well, she is her mother," he replies

"She's my mother too." I tell them. "But I won't love her she when she's never loved me. I have to put up with her crap while I live with her, but after I leave, I won't give her another thought. I cant understand why Misty still tries to make her care."

"She's seven." Wyatt states.

"Exactly. She should have learnt by now, like I did. Mum is never gonna change."

They don't understand. They've never had the chance to meet her. If I were to ever bring friends home, Mum would lose it. She'd throw them out and ground me for several years. Not that it means anything to me.

Misty and I never have permission to bring friends home, but Mum can invite every man she lays eyes on into her bed. It's no surprise she can't remember who either of our fathers are.

I've never considered inviting my friends over though. I never want them to meet my mother. They don't deserve that kind of torture.

"So, you'd leave her?" Axel asks.

"She wouldn't want to come with me," I explain. "She would want to stay even if Mum told her to get out."

I watch Jonah roll a soccer ball beneath his feet, kicking it around to himself at the end of the table.

Axel, sitting at the end of the seat, steals the ball from him with his feet and gets up. They fight back and forth for the ball, rolling it around between their legs.

Axel towers over him.

Jonah gets dealt all the short jokes despite him being five foot six and only two inches shorter than me and Wyatt.

His blonde hair begins to come loose and fall from the messy bun, so he pulls the hair tie out and lets it fall to his shoulders while trying to steal the ball back. I'm never used to seeing Jonah with his hair down. He's only ever taken it out to go swimming.

His contagious laugh brings smiles to all our faces like it does with everyone. The radiating joy can make him friends with anyone while his thick, muscular build will deter anyone from messing with him.

"You two coming?" Jonah asks, keeping his eyes on the ball, both of them making a slow migration to the field.

"I thought, maybe, I would have one of these first." I pull the pack of cigarettes out of the pocket of my jacket and hold them up for both of them to see.

"Seriously?" Axel asks, rolling his eyes, walking back to the table, leaving behind the ball. Jonah uses the time to tie his hair up on his way over.

"Hell yeah." I say, pulling out one of the four cigarettes left in the pack.

I offer one to Wyatt and Axel but they both decline. Jonah takes one and uses the orange lighter I stole from my mum a year ago to light it.

Like usual, I notice he takes a couple of puffs before letting the cigarette burn away in his fingers until he snuffs it out on the table. I don't mind. It's not costing me anything.

My body relaxes as soon as I take the first breath in of the smoke. The last pack I took ran out a week ago. I definitely needed this. After the long week my mother caused me to have, I needed something to help me relieve some stress.

The three of them made conversation while we smoke, but I'm too consumed by calm washing over me from the smoke to be bothered to join in.

The cigarette comes down to the end and I decide snuff the last of it out. We grab the ball on our way the field where we kick it around and play multiple silly and fun games while the sun sets.

Chapter 2

The sun sets. People settle into their homes. Still, we laugh and run. Play and shout. Find ways to keep ourselves entertained, and try out a few stupid ideas.

One game only involved an aim to knock each other off our feet, and another where we would throw several pinecones up into the darkness and try not to be hit by them as they fell back to the earth.

Tired, sweaty and sore, we walk back to our cars. In the carpark, I remember who I'm going home to, so I pull out the pack of cigarettes and place one of the two between my lips. Jonah spots me and asks for my last one, and I hand it over while internally annoyed at myself for not waiting for them to leave first. I hope I can steal more soon.

I pull out my phone as I shut my car door and gasp at the numbers that flash up on my blinding bright screen.

03:04

Below it, a notification reads '16 missed calls' from my mother. I roll my eyes and toss my phone onto the passenger seat, and start up my car in two attempts.

I drive the long way home and still pull into the driveway too soon for my liking. One look at the light on in the window, and I groan, taking my time getting out of the car.

Pausing for a second at the front door, I take a deep breath in, letting it out in a sigh, and push open the door.

"Where the hell have you been!"

"Why do you care?" I grumble, slamming the door shut.

"I've told you many times to be home by midnight!" She stands from the old lounge. "You're three hours late!"

"So?" I walk past her, towards the stairs, avoiding her death stare.

"So... I had plans tonight." She follows after me. Her white dress makes her skin look more orange than normal and forces her breasts to almost spill out over the top from how tight it is. I can't believe she thinks she looks good wearing that and is okay being seen in public wearing Barbie's outfit.

"Of course you did," I say under my breath.

"I needed you home to take care of Misty."

"I don't care."

She rushes ahead to stand in my way, but I move around her and keep walking. Grabbing my arm, she pulls me back, and anger boils inside of me.

"Don't touch me." I try to pull my arm away from her, but her grip tightens and she pulls me closer.

"You listen to me." She pulls me close. Droplets of spit hit my face. "When I say be home by midnight, you get home by midnight."

The red stilts she calls heels allows her to meet my eyeline and restricts me from towering over her. So, I lean in as close as I can to appear as threatening as possible. "You have no right to tell me what to do," I growl.

"Oh, yes I do." Her nails dig into my upper arm. "I am your mother."

"You're nothing like a mother."

"I have given you everything, the least you could do is act like you deserve it and do as I say."

"Given me everything?" I repeat, disbelief thick in my voice. "All you've done is make my life a living hell."

"Then, get out." She throws my arm back at me and points to the door. "If you're unhappy and you wanna make your own rules, then go find somewhere to live by yourself."

I want to walk out. I wish I could leave right now. Say, "Sure,"—no—"Happy to," and never see her again. She would watch me walk out, with nothing left to say. But I can't. I haven't saved up enough to survive on my own yet.

I stay quiet a little too long and she takes the win. "Exactly," she says, "Now, shut your mouth, and get up to bed."

Without another word, I make my way towards the stairs.

I spot Misty at the bottom, peering around the corner. At the same time, Mum shouts, "Misty! You're supposed to be asleep! Get up to bed! Now!"

She disappears behind the wall, without uttering a sound. I hear her little feet plop up each step, and when I round the corner, I find her at the top already.

I stomp upstairs, breathing heavy, annoyed that I let the argument end that way. When I hear the front door open and slam shut,

I roll my eyes and sigh. Turns out I didn't ruin your plans after all, I think.

The sound of me slamming my door echoes around my small room. I fumble across the room, using my hands to guide me through the darkness, and I don't bother to change out of my clothes as I climb under the covers of my single sized bed.

Several seconds pass, when light filling my room alerts me to my door being opened. I wait a moment for Mum to yell at me once more, but when the room stays silent, I roll over and come face to face with a wide-eyed Misty. Better than being face to face with Mum, I guess.

"Why were you and Mummy yelling?"

"Because she's mean." I roll back over, and close my eyes, hoping she takes the hint.

"I don't like it when you yell at her."

"She yells at me too." How can she be so blinded about Mum?

"Yeah, but-"

I cut her off. "Misty, go to bed."

Silence fills my room and I wait for the sound of the door shutting.

"Will she bring someone home tonight?" I jerk in surprise at the closeness of her voice.

"Yep." Why won't she leave? Let me sleep.

"Why does she-"

"Go to bed, Misty," I order her, raising my voice.

"Can I sleep in here?" she asks, her voice almost too quiet to hear.

"No," I tell her. "You have your own bed."

"But, I had a bad dream-" The mattress droops from her weight leaning on my bed.

"I don't care. Go away."

"But-"

I flip over to glare at her, her small face hidden by shadows. "Get out."

Her sparkling eyes flick back and forth between mine, shrinking back. "Fine." I wait until she walks out and closes the door before I flop back down on my pillow.

Finally. Thank God.

I don't want to hear about her opinion on the argument. I don't need her to blame it all on me. I don't care that—if she thinks Mum did nothing wrong. She's wrong. Mum's not the saint she thinks she is. She needs to grow up and see that already.

I wasn't—she—Mum was the one—she hurt me. She was—she was getting in my face. She was yelling just as much—she was yelling more than me. She started the yelling. Does Misty see that? No. She never sees—she only ever sees me. What I do to Mum. That's all she sees.

This is why I could never take Misty with me when I leave. She doesn't care about me. She cares about Mum. Mum's the one she loves. Mum's the one she—she wants to hang around. She always picks Mum's side. I practically raised her, and still she wants her.

Well, she can have her. I can live without both of them. Mum doesn't want me, and I don't want her. And if Misty keeps choosing Mum, I don't want her either. If—when I leave, if I took Misty with me, she would just complain about me and pick our mother, like she does now.

I don't want that. I don't need them. One day, I'll get out of here and I'll never look back. I won't miss a thing. I ll be on my own. Free.

Slam!

My body jerks awake. I don't remember drifting off to sleep.

Soft light filters in through my thin, see-through curtains.

Mum's voice drifts up from downstairs. I can't make out a single word, but somehow I can tell she's drunk.

When the muffled voice of my mother stops and a deeper voice carries through the house, I know she's been successful in finding a desperate guy to bring home.

They don't spend long in the kitchen or lounge area. The conversation stays short and I can tell my mum's replies are curt.

I listen to the mumbling as it echoes up the stairs and down the hall until I hear them close the door to my mother's bedroom door. The house falls quiet again.

For a second, I consider going down there to ruin her fun. To do something that would disturb the wonderful night she has planned. But the only thing I can think of that could do that would be to get the guy to leave. That would ruin her night. Except I don't know how I could achieve that.

Kick him out? He wouldn't listen to me. Start an argument with Mum. Make it awkward enough to make him want to get away. I'm too tired to argue though.

Nothing would work. There's no reason to drag myself from my bed. Even if I had a plan, exhaustion holds me down in my bed.

I push Mum into the furthermost part of my mind, and instead, play out scenarios of moving out until I drift into away into a dreamless sleep.

CHAPTER 3

The cold shower brings me comfort. As the water washes over my head, and down my entire body to my feet, I relax and let my mind empty.

While I get dressed, I listen for sounds from downstairs. Anything that could let me know if I have to face Mum before I leave. I stay as quiet as possible and tread with soft steps on the wooden floors. On the way down, I avoid the stairs I know will squeak.

At the bottom of the stairs, and outside her door, I hear her loud snores. Knowing I'll be faster out the door than she'll be out of bed, I forget about tip-toeing the rest of the way.

As I walk past the counter, an old, half-torn piece of paper catches my eye. Scrawled on it in thick black pen reads:

DORIANDO NOT LEAVE THIS HOUSE! YOUR GROUNDEDYOU NEED TO WATCH MISTY TODAY

I scrunch the paper up in my hand and toss it across the kitchen bench. Ignoring her pathetic threat, I walk out.

If I were her, I would have given up trying to ground me years ago, but she still thinks she stands a chance. I want to laugh. She has no chance at keeping me here.

I drive the familiar route to the basketball courts and pull up to find Axel and Wyatt already there, tossing the basketball between each other.

I'm greeted by them and soon after, Jonah arrives. We dish out insults and criticism for being late like they all did to me yesterday, despite him arriving only a minute after me.

After a few jokes and short conversations, Jonah steals the ball from Wyatt and runs onto the court. "Come on," he says. "Let's go losers. Who's on my team?"

"I dibs Wyatt's team!" Axel shouts, and I smile and roll my eyes. I wonder how Wyatt feels to have the three of us always fighting to be on his team, since we all know Wyatt has the skill to win in any sport.

Like always, our game starts off normal, but when Jonah and I start losing, we ruin the proper game and do whatever it takes to get points. While Axel dribbles down the court, Jonah stops defending him and picks him up around the waist instead. He runs him all the way back to the other end and drops him off on the ground. While Axel laughs, Jonah snatches the ball from his grasp and throws it to me.

Before it reaches me, Wyatt jumps in front of me and catches it. He runs it to his hoop without dribbling once and throws it from the three point line, sinking it with ease.

We decide to end that game and switch partners to start another. In the first ten minutes, Wyatt makes his fifth shot while Axel and I fail to get a single point. After the sixth, the game becomes chaos.

I get the in the ball and when Jonah tries to defend me, I turn and run the other way. We run half way across the park and only stop when we reach the fence around the courts and field.

After three hours, a phone rings from the bench holding our stuff. I recognise my ringtone and head over to it while the others fool around. During the short walk, my body becomes very tense with my suspicion on the name I will see. I near the table, spot the name 'EVIL', and I turn and walk away without picking up the phone.

"Your Mum?" Wyatt asks, and I give him a nod.

We start playing while the ringing continues. When it stops, my muscles relax and I put my focus into the game, but seconds later the ringtone plays again and the game comes to a halt.

"You wanna answer it?" Johan asks through his harsh breaths.

"Hell no," I reply, and with a nod from me, the game continues.

The ringing stops. Axel takes the ball from Jonah, and the tone plays again.

"I think it's important, mate," Axel says, holding the ball in his hands. "Maybe you should get it."

"It's never important," I tell them. "She just wants to yell at me for leaving the house."

"Maybe you should answer it anyway," Jonah suggests. "Just to get her off your back."

"She's never off my back. Answering a phone won't change that."

"True."

After that, we let the phone ring and listen to the tune play over and over and over again until I can't stand it anymore and I turn my phone off.

Two hours later, at four in the afternoon, we decide to all head home, but not before making an arrangement to meet up at the Jonah's house for dinner while his parents are away.

"See ya in a couple of hours," we say, but I know I'll get there sooner just to get away from Mum.

Getting in my car, I turn my phone on and sigh when the notifications show up. Ten missed phone calls. Fourteen messages. Six voicemails. The first message reads, "GET HOME NKW!!!"

Tossing my phone onto the passenger seat, I start my car and pull out onto the road. As I do, the phone rings for the eleventh time. I let it ring, face down on the seat, knowing very well who it will be.

I only have to deal with listening to my ringtone one more time during the fifteen minute trip home.

Pulling up into the driveway, I consider changing my ringtone later, and I think I'll change the ringtone for Mum to something silent.

I snatch my phone up and get out of the car, bracing myself for the explosive outburst that I'll get before I can step inside. One last deep breath in and I push the door open.

I stand frozen in the doorway, staring at the scene in front of me. Fear and shock grips my heart. What happened? Did she seriously throw this big of a tantrum about me leaving?

Chairs lie on their sides. Papers litter the ground. The disgusting, cream-coloured pillows from the couch have been tossed all around the house. Pieces of shattered dirty plates from the sink spread across the entire floor.

I step over the coffee table laid on its side in front of the doorway, looking around at the chaos within the small room. The glass and plate chips crunch beneath my shoes. Papers flutter and drift around the room from the fan spinning on the ceiling.

How—Wha—What happened? She's never—never done anything like this before. Did she finally snap? Why? What did it? Was it—could it have been Misty? What would—could she have done—something worse than I've ever done—what could she have done to make Mum do this?

Where was Misty during all of this? Did she stay in her room? I hope she did. I hope she's not hurt. I don't want to play doctor.

Stepping over everything, I get to the stairs and dash up them. Halfway up, I hear a door open from behind me and I stop, looking back down.

"Dorian!?" Mum's voice calls from out of sight.

As I move back down the stairs, she steps out from around the corner, looking up at me. "Where have you been?" I expected more anger and volume in her voice. I've never heard her talk so quiet.

"With friends." I step down until I'm on the last step, standing in her face and above her. I hold myself tall.

"Did you not hear any of my phone calls?" She turns away and moves towards the kitchen counter, compelling me to scrunch my face up in confusion. What's up with her?

"No, I heard them."

"Did you read my messages?"

I watch her pick a smoke out of a new pack, and hold it between her lips as she lights the end. The question repeats in my head. Her calm tone unnerves me so much I forget to answer for a moment. "Uh—N-no."

"Maybe you should have?" Smoke wafts out of her mouth with her words. She walks back to her room, leaving me alone, confused, and in shock. Her door closes.

I pull my phone out from my pocket and open up the messages from 'EVIL'. I scroll up to the earlier messages and read them from top to bottom.

"Where are you"

"I told you not to leave!!"

"Dont bother coming back"

"ehat have yoh done!!!"

"did you come hime"

"Where are uou"

"Do you have Misty"

"Answer me!!"

"DORIAN. PICK YP YOUR PHONE!!!"

"WHAT HALPENED"

"andwer my valls"

"Dorian"

"DORIAN"

"GET HOME NKW!!!"

By the end, my mind whirls around at top speed. Each message whips around inside my skull, refusing to slow down to be processed. It takes me several minutes make sense of them all. I stand in the same spot, reading and re-reading each text over and over again.

After the fifth time, I notice my harsh, shallow breaths causing my head to spin even more. I grab the railing attached to the wall and shut my eyes.

What does this mean?

Opening them again, I look down at the screen. One message stands out at me.

"Do you have Misty"

What did she mean by that? Misty is here, at home. Why would I take her? Where else could she be, besides here?

Chapter 4

I dash around the corner and burst through the door to my mother's bedroom to find her on her queen-sized bed. Propped up by pillows behind her back. Sucking on her cigarette. Her eyes glued to the TV sitting on the dresser. She doesn't glance over at me and doesn't make eye contact until I block her view of whatever crap TV show she's watching.

"What?" she says.

"What did you mean by, do I have Misty?" My heart pounds against my chest. "Isn't she here?"

"Nah," she says, trying to peer around me to continue watching, but I step sideways and block her view. "Don't know where that girl is."

What?! "What happened?"

"Uh," she groans. "Well, I left for some cigarettes." She glares at me. "Because someone took my last pack, and when I got back home, she was gone."

"Gone where?"

"How am I supposed to know." She flicks her hand at me, telling me to get out her way of the TV program.

"Because she's your kid," I yell. "She's your responsibility." Anger burns like fire in my veins.

She reaches her hand out to the white ceramic ashtray resting on her wooden bedside-table, and flicks the ash off the end. "I needed cigarettes."

"So, you just left her home alone?" My voice bounces off ever wall.

"No, I left her with Nathan."

I scrunch my brows together, repeating the name in my head, searching for someone I know named Nathan. A neighbour? Relative? No. "Who's that?"

"The guy from last night."

My heart skips a beat. "Are you serious! Where did he take her?"

She sighs and rolls her eyes. "I don't know."

"Did you call the cops?" She called me. She better have called the cops too.

"No."

"No?! Why not? How do you plan on finding her?"

"I don't know. He'll probably bring her back."

"And if he doesn't?"

"I don't know, Dorian! Now, get out of the way."

A gasp escapes my mouth. She can't be serious. Her daughter is missing and all she cares about is watching TV.

Huffing air out of my nose like an angry bull, I turn and press the power button on the TV.

I whip back around to be hit by her furious glare. She sits up on her bed. "Turn it back on and and get out."

"Step up and be a real mother." I grind my teeth together to the point where I worry about them shattering into pieces from the pressure.

"Don't talk to me about being a mother!" She gets to her feet, walking to the end of the bed. "I've done everything for you two and—"

"You've done nothing," I scream. "You're still doing nothing!" I clench my fists at my sides. "You're daughter has been taken and you're doing nothing to get her back! Do something!"

She puts the cigarette to her mouth and I have to resist the urge to rip it from fingers and toss it to the floor. "For all I know, she wanted to leave."

"What?!" Does she honestly believe she left willingly while the house looks like it's been raided?

"Well, she's been begging me for years to take her to that water park. She probably begged Nathan to take her, and he did."

"Or he kidnapped her!"

"What am I supposed to do about that?" How could she be so cruel? Why did we get stuck with a mother that only cares about herself?

"Call the cops!" Heat flushes through my body. I unclench my hands to wipe my sweaty palms on my pants. She's hopeless. Irresponsible. She's relaxing while her child is God-knows-where.

"Yeah, I'll do that and then she come home safe and sound; all excited that got to go to the water park."

I can't fathom her selfishness and cold heart. with every word out of her mouth, my heart breaks more and more. "How can you not be worried?! Why don't you ever care?!" A pang hits my chest, aching from my heart and through every rib.

"Get out, Dorian."

The edges of my vision blur with brimming tears. I scream, "Why are you so heartless?!"

"I am not heartless!" She steps closer, waving the cigarette in my face. "You try dealing with two snot-nosed kids that never appreciate what you've done for them."

"What have you done for me, Mum? Tell me."

"I gave up everything for you two. I used to be able to enjoy life until you ungrateful kids came along."

"It was your choice to have kids!"

"It wasn't planned. I never wanted either of you."

A pain I've never experienced before hits the centre of my heart. I've felt unwanted and unloved by her for years, but hearing he say the words breaks the remainder of my heart. I step backwards, hitting the dresser. The TV rocks on its stand. I don't care if it falls over and breaks.

I knew she didn't love us, but I never thought I would hear her admit it.

I stare at her face. Anticipating—wishing—for even a flicker of guilt or regret. Nothing I get nothing.

I search for a reply. Something I could say to hurt her as much as she hurt me. I want her to break like I have. She deserves to feel unwanted and unloved. The pain might actually crack the stone that surrounds her heart. Nothing comes close. Nothing will ever come close. She out-did herself and brought me to my knees.

The silence gnaws at me. Eating me alive. She doesn't utter a word. I'm stuck in a stunned stupor.

The smoke from her cigarette rises between us.

"Get out of the way," she says.

I stand like stone, determined not to give her what she wants.

"Move, Dorian."

Not happening. She needs to know what it's like to be defeated.

"I'm not going to tell you again. Leave."

I straighten up, making myself taller and bigger. Misty could need her mother right now and she doesn't have a reliable one.

My mother purses her lips together and squares her shoulders. Before I can blink, I'm shoved to the side.

I stumble sideways until I crash into the wall, crushing my shoulder and I take a knock to my head.

Without another word, she switches the TV back on and walks back to the bed. I stare in disbelief. How does she do it? How did she rid herself of any sympathy?

As she makes herself comfortable in bed, my muscles twitch and tense, and an idea pops into my head. I duck out of room and into the kitchen. The clanging sound of metal echoes through the house as I rummage through every drawer, slamming them shut when my search comes up empty.

Where are they? Why can I never find anything in this house?

Bang! I look over my shoulder to see my mother's door shut.

I really hate her. I hope she—Found them! I storm back into the room with a mission.

I know this won't end well, but I don't care. I'll take whatever she dishes out.

Throwing the door back to slam against the same wall I hit, I stomp over to the TV.

"What are you doing?" She gets out of bed, panic lacing her voice.

I pick up the power cord, rip it out from the wall, and without any hesitation, I cut it with the scissors. The screen goes black and the room falls silent. Before I can turn around, I'm pushed to the side again, only this time I'm able to save myself and I whip around with a stern, angry look.

Chapter 5

"What have you done?!" Her hand flies towards me. I try to block the strike but with my late reaction, I'm forced to take the hit on my upper arm. "Why the bloody hell would you do that?!" She goes in for another hit, but I'm able to dodge it this time by stepping backwards.

"Misty needs you!" I take a step forward, but stay alert for another swing that could come my way.

"There's nothing I can do," she says.

"Call! The! Cops! Find Nathan! Anything more than watching TV would be great." My voice rips at my throat.

She shakes her head. "What would the cops do?"

"More than you!"

"She'll be fine!" She waves her hand at me. "We don't need to call the cops. I'm sure she'll come home later when she's done running around the town."

"You don't have to trust the cops, just call them." I hiss my words through my clenched teeth. "They won't find whatever you've stolen. They'll find her." Misty should be more important to her than her secret stash.

"Stop telling me what to do!" Her smoke drifts into my face, swirling in front of my vision, and getting on my nerves.

"I will, when you do something to get Misty back."

She moves her face closer to mine, spitting her words at me. "Why don't you do something?"

"That's not my job." Fed up with the smoke wafting between us, I snatch her cigarette out of her fingers. "You're the mother!" I throw it on the ground. "Act like one!" Stomping my foot down on it snuffs the embers out and puts an end to the continuous line of smoke.

She looks down at it and when she looks up at me again, her eyes darken; fire raging behind her expression. "Get out!" She thrusts the heel of her hands into my chest, shoving me out the door. "Get out of the house! If you want her, go find her!"

Fighting back, I do what I can to stop her, but I'm only able to get her off me when I step out of the room. I jump forward to keep her from slamming the door shut. She pushes against it and I do the same, but with the door almost closed, she has the upper hand. As it closes, I have to rip my fingers away before they can get crushed.

The door shuts and I hear the lock click. I'm left standing in the unused dining area. Alone, listening to my pounding heart and harsh breathing. I spin around, taking in my surroundings.

What would have caused this? Was it—what's-his-name—Nathan? Or did Misty do all this? Why would she throw—

An icy cold hand grips my heart. Tingles crawl over my scalp, spilling down to my shoulders, racing through my spine. What—what did he do to her? To make her—She was left alone—left alone with him. He could have done anything. Did he try to hurt her? Why else would she trash the house and throw things, if not to defend herself?

Why would he take her? Why—What would make him want her? A thought pops into my head, tying my stomach into knots. He wouldn't—he couldn't—please—please not for any sexual reason—or—or—What if he's dangerous? He could kill her.

My stomach swirls. A burning liquid rises in my throat. I rush to the kitchen sink, but by the time I make it there, the bile had sunk back down. The bitter taste remains on my tongue, and I hold my mouth under the running tap to wash it out.

With my hands on the edge of the counter holding me up, I stare between the disgusting yellow curtains either side of the small window. I'm not focused on anything in particular: I'm lost in thought.

I need to get her back. She's probably in serious trouble with him. I can't—I won't just leave her with him, like Mum plans to. I have to get her back.

How do I find him though? I don't even know what he looks like. Or his last name. I know nothing about him. Where do I start? What do I do? How do I do it? I don't have any information to give the cops if I call them. Mum needs to do it, but she's useless.

If the cops turn up here, she won't talk to them. She won't even come out of her room. She would probably jump through her window just to avoid the police. She hates police. Says they're all corrupt. Out to get anyone they can. It's never been a problem before, but it just became a big one.

Should I just call the police anyway? If I do, what do I tell them? I don't have any information to give them. I have half a name. That's it. It wouldn't be enough.

If I gave the police his name, what would they do with it? Start n investigation? An investigation would take too long, wouldn't it? Does she have that time to wait? Would they be too late? Is it already too late?

I pull the beanie off my head, letting it drop to the floor, and tug at my hair with my trembling fingers. Pressure builds on my chest, threatening to suffocate me. My head spins like a tornado. Around and around, making me ill. I let out a slow shaky breath, trying and failing to organise my thoughts.

My eyes dart around the room, frantically searching for a clue to anything. Something to lead me in a direction. Nothing stands out to me.

Maybe something upstairs could give me an idea. I dash up the stairs, taking three at a time, rushing down the hallway and into her room on the right.

As I rush in, I notice my door swung open. I make sure I close my door every time I leave it. Ignoring it for now, I duck into her room and gasp.

I'm used to her room being a mess, but never this bad. She always has toys lying all over the floor but now there's more than that. Clothes hang over the open drawers and cover the floor. Her bedsheets on her single-sized bed have been pulled down and her two pillows sit on the floor on the opposite side of the room.

The wall that holds all the pictures she drew looks strange with several of them missing, and I can't find them anywhere on the floor as I scan the area.

Items drape and stick out of her large cupboard opposite her bed. One light pink curtain hangs down from the curtain rod, attached by a single hook not ripped down.

The tiny TV still plays some kind of program on low volume.

I step into the room, tip-toeing around items. Circling the room, I notice a few more things I know to be missing.

The pile of school books and papers on the floor draws my attention to her missing backpack. I also can't find the first thing I knew to look for. Her small, dirty, pink stuffed rabbit. She carries it with her everywhere she goes in the house. However, she hates taking out of the house, because she doesn't want to lose him. She'll take him to sleepovers but not to a trip into town, and I'm certain she wouldn't have taken it to the water park like Mum thought.

Her blue jewellery box that usually sits on top of her dresser has left an empty spot. Several pieces of jewellery lie scattered on the edge of the dresser. I know it's not all of her jewellery. I know she took at least one. The one I gave her.

A silver bracelet with fake purple diamantes that I gave her for her fifth birthday. She wore it everyday for six months until we got into a big fight and I never saw her wear it again. I know she kept it, but now it's not here.

I don't have the time to sort through her clothes to check if some has been taken, I just assume that's the case.

With nothing left to find, I leave, making my way to my room, directly opposite Misty's. I don't have to step out of Misty's room to see into my room and I'm almost too shocked to get out the doorway.

Mine's not as bad as Misty's but seeing all my stuff thrown all over the place still irritates me. I know I can't blame Misty for it. It would be Nathan's fault.

I like to keep all my stuff pretty organised. Seeing everything on my floor really gets under my skin and I want to find this guy more than ever. I've told Misty a million times to stay out of my room when I'm not home, and she always listens. If she went in there without permission, it would have been to escape.

I give my floor a quick scan and rush down the hallway when nothing stands out to me from the mess.

The bathroom at the end of the hall remains quite organised, with the only exception being the two bowls with our hygiene products that have been spilled into the sink.

I place the black ceramic bowls back in their places on either side of the sink and start packing stuff back into them. Sorting and searching as I start piling in my deodorant, razor, shaving cream, comb, and floss. In doing so, I notice the absence of all of Misty's stuff.

Misty's purple toothbrush and her pink toothpaste can't be found as I dig through the contents. Her princess hairbrush and a few of her hair clips and hair ties are also missing, as well as the moisturiser she got from a friend that she loves to apply to her face and arms.

I dump the rest of the items I have in my hands back into the sink and walk out. Before I leave, I spot the crack running up the doorframe and pull back to a stop. Something cold and sharp grips my heart at the sight. Checking the door, I notice the splintered wood I never saw upon entering. He kicked the door in to get her.

My teeth grind together and push the door back into the wall as I stomp out.

Why the hell did he take her, and why did he pack for her first?

I fly down the hallway and scamper down the stairs, rounding the corner to pound on the door of the only person who could give me any answers.

Chapter 6

Bang! Bang! Bang! Bang! Bang! I don't stop until the door swings open to reveal my red-faced mother.

"Walk away now!"

"Who was he?" I ask, ignoring her threat.

"Go away!" She tries to close the door but my hand slams against it, forcing it back open again. I won't let her win this time.

"What do you know about him?"

She shoots daggers at me with her eyes. "Why do you want to know?"

"Because, unlike you, I'm going to find her."

Her eyes widen, and her jaw falls open. "You're going to find her? Ha." Her head flops back. "You're useless at everything you do."

A small pang hits my heart. "At least I care."

"No, you don't," she fires back. "Because if you did, you wouldn't have left this morning when I told you not to!"

"You left too." I jab a finger at her. "Only you left her alone with a stranger."

"Yeah, because you stole my smokes." She waves her hand in front of me and I spot the new smoke in her hand. "If you hadn't of done that, I wouldn't have needed to leave."

"Stop blaming me!"

"Why? It's your fault," she scoffs, waving her arms around. "You knew you had to watch Misty today. I know you read my note because you left it scrunched up on the counter." She glares at me. "You didn't care. You left."

"So, did you!" Why can't she get it? I left Misty with her mother, she left Misty with a stranger. There's a difference. "And you brought the guy into the house! You're the one who put her in danger!"

"Because you stole my smokes!"

A layer of sweat covers my entire body. "That's no reason to leave your child behind!" Heat flushes through my body.

"I was coming back!" she tells me, as if that make it any better.

"Yeah, but you were already too late!"

She clenches her jaw and flares her nostrils. "So were you!" she shouts. "You couldn't even pick up your phone. What's the point of you having one?" Her face reddens the more she yells and spit flies out of her mouth with each word. "If you had followed my orders for the first time in your life and stayed home like you should have, this wouldn't had happened."

"If you weren't so selfish–" I begin.

"Look who's talking about being selfish." She laughs.

I furrow my brows at her. "You chose smokes over your daughter!"

"And you choose yourself over everything, always."

A silence stretches between us as I search for a come back while glaring at her. I can't get over how awful and selfish she is. I hate her.

"You weren't here," she continues, "because you only care about yourself. That's why everything happened."

"No," I say, "Everything happened because your a incompetent, self-centred, lousy mother that doesn't deserve to have children." I watch her eyes widen and she sucks in a breath. "You're useless and cruel. You've never loved anyone but yourself. You've never done anything for the family. You don't deserve the title of mother."

A burning sting swells in my left cheek and I have to let my brain process the scene in front of me before I can understand what happened.

I hold my cheek in my palm and stare at my mother with absolute shock. I'm used to her shoving me and dragging me around, but she's never hit me.

"If you ever talk to me like that again—" She closes the gap between us, talking through her clenched teeth and glaring at me through her squinted angry eyes. "—you'll regret it."

I stand frozen to the floor, my eyes flicking frantically between hers.

She grips the front of my shirt and for the first time in my life, a slight panic for my mother's actions sends shivers over my skin.

"I am the boss under this roof," she continues, "you will find some respect and treat me with it. Or you will get out." Releasing her grip, she shoves me backwards. "If you want to find that little brat and bring her back, fine, but don't come to me for help."

"Why did he take her?" I ask.

"What did I just say?" she says, throwing her hands up.

"You're the only one who knows him," I tell her. "So, either answer my questions or I'm calling the cops and you can answer their questions."

She draws in a breath and releases it in a long harsh sigh. crossing her arms—keeping her fingers holding her smoke away from her—she gives me a defeated look, but stays silent.

I repeat my question. "Why did he take her?"

"Because he wanted an annoying child to pester him about unimportant things." Sarcasm drips from her tongue.

Grinding my teeth and glaring at her, I pull out my phone from my back jeans pocket.

"How am I supposed to know why he wanted her?!" she shouts at me, her eyes staring at the phone.

I hold up the phone, showing the number pad, ready to type. "Where does he live?"

"I don't know."

"What's his last name?"

"I don't know."

"Did you talk to him at all?" My rising voice cracks at the end, and I clear my throat before continuing. "Or did you two head straight to the bedroom?"

"We didn't swap life stories," she tells me, sucking on her smoke.

"You have to know something." Giving it a little bit of thought, I ask, "Where did you meet him?"

"Dale's Pub."

I let my hand drop and shake my head. "What else?"

She gives me a half-hearted shrug.

"You have to know something else," I say, "Anything."

She disappears into her mind, already shaking her head, telling me no. He wrinkles smooth over and her head stills. After a brief pause, she looks me in the eye and says, "No."

Liar. "Tell me."

Rolling her eyes, she says, "He said we had met before."

"When?"

"I don't remember him."

"Of course you don't," I say under my breath.

"Watch it," she warns me, jabbing a finger towards me. "He said we had a night together about eight years ago, back when we were still living in that house on Clove Street."

I think back to those times, unable to picture who it could be amongst the many faces I can barely remember, but no one specific comes to mind.

"Apparently, we spent a month together," she continues, "and then I told him I was done, and we haven't seen each other since."

"You spent a month together and you don't remember him?"

"He's nothing special," she shrugs.

I roll my eyes, shake my head and give a quiet sigh. "What happened before you left this morning?"

"I woke up," she explains, "came out to the kitchen and started making breakfast."

"And then..." I encourage her to continue.

"And then he came out, asked if he could eat something, and I said yes."

"And..."

"He asked me why I was irritated," she says, smugly, pausing to suck on her cigarette one last time before she leans forward and snuffs out the end on the small kitchen table. "And I told him it was because my good-for-nothing son refused to follow my orders and took off to do whatever he likes."

I roll my eyes at her.

"He mentioned that he remembered you from the first time we were together and that he would love to meet you now. I told him it would be the biggest disappointment of his life."

Sick of her belittling, I growl at her, "Did he meet Misty before you left?"

"Yeah," she replies, as if she didn't just tear me down. "She came down for breakfast not too long after that and they sat there talking and talking and talking." She taps her thumb to her fingers, imitating their non-stop conversation. I know Misty can talk anyone's ear off but Mum's definition of a lengthy conversation is one that lasts more than two sentences.

"About what?" I ask.

"I don't know," she sighs.

"Think." I hold my phone up, only letting my arm drop when it's done its job.

She glares at me a moment and says, "He asked what her name was. She told him. Then, he asked what her rabbit was called. She told him everything there was to know about it." Her eyes roll. "He asked her how old she was, when her birthday was, and whether or not she got that ratty old rabbit as a birthday gift."

She stops, her eyes asking me if that's enough.

"Keep going," I answer her unspoken question.

"She told him she got it when she was four, and they talked more about it but I didn't pay attention to the rest."

"Do you remember anything else they talked about?" I need more. She's given me nothing. A doctor in a graveyard would be more useful than her.

"No."

My jaw clenches. I lift the phone back up into her view.

Sighing, she tosses her head back. "She mentioned the water park at one point and he told her about the park his nephew—or someone—enjoys. She said she wanted to go there after she went to the water park and I wanted to slap him right then and there." Her voice echoes throughout the house. "She ran upstairs and brought back her pencils and colouring books and they sat at the counter colouring until I kicked them off and they moved to the couch." Annoyance coats her voice like syrup on a pancake.

"What else did they talk about?" I press on.

She rolls her eyes, looking more and more impatient with every question I ask. "He asked her what her favourite food is and of course she said ice cream. He said something about milkshakes and she mentioned that she doesn't remember ever having one." She gives it a little more thought without me having to force her. "I remember him asking her about her last holiday," she scoffs, "and they were talking about hiking and and going on adventures."

"And..." My impatience grows thinner each time she stops. Just keep going and get it out with already. Why does she have to be so frustrating?

"I told them I was going to get a pack of cigarettes and that I'd be back in five minutes. Then, I left." She lays stress on her last words, making it clear she's done with all she knows. Or so she thinks.

"Did he mention any plans he had?" I ask, enjoying the sight of pressing her lips together in annoyance. "Any clue as to where he might have gone with her?"

"No." Her blunt tone has no effect on me.

I give her a fake smirk. "Very helpful."

"Is the interrogation done now?"

"Yeah," I tell her, making a shooing motion with my hand at her. "Go and enjoy your alone time."

"Pathetic parasite," she says under her breath while walking back into her bedroom.

I ignore her remark, brushing it off like everything else she's ever said to me.

As she begins to close her door, I realise I still have nothing to help me. "Wait," I shout, stopping her in her tracks. I need more.

With a long groan, she opens the door, leaning against it. "What?" she whines.

"You have to know something about him. More than just his name. His last name, address, phone number. Some—thing. Where he works. You can't possibly only know his first name."

Her head flops to the side, giving me an exasperated look. "Yeah," she says with a sigh. "He gave me his number."

What? "Why would you leave that out? Give it to me," I order.

"If I give it to you, will you leave me alone."

"Yeah, sure."

She wanders back into her room, leaving the door open. I follow her but stop in the doorway, watching her lean down to the small plastic bin in the corner of her room. Reaching in, she holds something inside her hand, and makes her way back to me.

She holds up a piece of crumpled paper. As I reach for it, she pulls it back. "You won't involve the police?" I know it's a question but she found a way to make it sound like a order.

"Not if you give it to me," I tell her, holding my hand out.

With a sigh, she slaps the paper down into my hand.

"Is that it?"

First, I unfold the paper to check she hasn't lied to me. "Yeah," I tell her, and she steps backwards, slamming the door shut so hard the vibrations can be felt around the entire house.

I type the number into my phone and double check the digits. Hitting the call button, I put the phone to my ear.

CHAPTER 7

I attempt to calm my out of control breathing as the phone connects to his, but focusing on it makes it worse. Pressure builds up below my ears from my tense jaw and my head begins to pound from a headache growing behind my eyes. The ring starts and I listen to that instead.

Brr, brr. Brr, brr. Brr, b-

A man's voice answers. "Hello?"

I unclench my jaw and clear my throat. "Hello, is—is this Nathan?" I ask, calmer than I would like.

"Yes," he replies, confusion lacing his scratchy voice. "Who is this?"

I straighten up and square my shoulders, despite him not being able to see me. My voice a deep rumble like rolling thunder, I reply, "I believe you have my sister."

A short intake of breath echoes through the speaker, and then silence. It stretches on for what seems like forever, until a beeping sound echoes through, and the call ends.

"Coward," I growl under my breath, pulling the phone away from my ear. I bash the button with my thumb and the ring screen pops back up. The phone slams against my ear and I hear the buzzing ring. He takes longer to answer, and for a moment I'm certain I'll go straight to his voicemail.

When the ringing stops, I speak before he can. "Where is she?

"She's safe," he tells me.

I hiss into the phone, "That wasn't the question." The rising anger warms me from head to toe, and beads of sweat drip from my hairline.

"She's with me." His refusal to answer the question tenses every muscle in my body.

"She shouldn't be with you," I growl. "Bring her back." I squeeze the phone in my hand until it shakes against my ear.

"She's safe with me."

"I don't care!" I shout down the speaker. "She doesn't belong to you." My voice shakes with rage.

"She does now."

Chills erupt over my entire body, fizzling down every nerve and vein, finishing at the end of my fingers and toes. My stomach flips and wraps itself into a knot. Nausea seeps into my gut and swirls around like a tornado.

Pain settles in my jaw from the tension I create. As I stare at the small oval table in front of me, my quivering muscles yearn to send it fly across the room, and I have to dig my heels into the ground to resist.

"No, she doesn't," I snarl. "Bring her back now, or I'm calling the cops."

"Her mother is not fit to take care of her."

How would he know? He's only known Misty existed for a couple of hours, and he's spent only one night with Mum in the past six years. He knows nothing!

Anger surges through me, igniting every nerve ending and twitching every muscle. "That's not your call to make." My feet move me, unable to stand still for any longer. I pace the room up and down, kicking everything that gets in my way.

"It is," he says. "She's told me everything she's not allowed to do and the way she's treated. No child should live like that." His rough voice gets under my skin.

I agree our mother is the worst mother in history. She doesn't care about her children or anyone who isn't herself, and she has never done anything a mother should do for her children, but that's no excuse for him to kidnap a child.

"It's none of your business," I say, sending a piece of shattered plate flying across the room with my shoe, causing it to smash into the wall beside the front door.

"I've made it my business," he says.

"Too bad," I snap. "Give her back."

"I can't do that," he tells me.

"Yes, you can," I say, "and you will!" My voice bounces around the room.

"Shut up," I hear my mother yell from inside her bedroom, but I ignore her.

"No," he says, raising his voice to keep up with my constant rising tone. "I'll take care of her and raise her the right way."

"That's not your responsibility!" I scream at him.

Retreating back to the comfort of his regular tone, he says, "It is."

"Says who?" I say through gritted teeth.

"I do," he replies.

I scoff at him. "And who do you think you are?"

The conversation comes to a standstill for just a moment, as if someone hit pause on a remote. I hear a sharp intake of breath through the speaker and stop pacing as I hear him take his time to release it . My patience grows thin waiting for his reply, and just as I'm about to scream at him to answer, he does.

"I'm her father."

CHAPTER 8

S hivers rush over my skin. "Wh—What?" I couldn't have heard that right.

"I'm her father," he repeats.

My brain struggles to find the words. "I- er- what-" I shake my head, attempting to clear my thoughts. "How do you figure that?"

"She told me her birthday," he explains. "I calculated it and figured out she would have been conceived during the time her mum and I were together."

"Do you know how many men she's slept with?" I tell him. "She was probably sleeping with five other guys at the same time as you." The line goes quiet and I jump at the opportunity as an insult pops in my head and I speak loud enough for Mum to hear through her closed door. "She's such a whore, she's run out of men to sleep with and has made a full circle and started bringing home men she already slept with eight years ago."

"She deserves someone who actually loves her," he replies, "and her mother won't do that. I will." His voice becomes rougher as anger filters into his words.

"Dorian," Misty says in the background. My heart leaps but my stomach sinks. The panic and fear bleeds through her quiet voice.

Before I can get a word out, the beeps cut me off, letting me know the call has ended.

I scream, balling my free hand up into a fist and crushing my phone in my hand. My eyes squeeze shut and I curl over, letting it all out.

Straightening up, I tap on the number again and listen to it ring.

Brr, brr. Brr, brr. Brr, brr. It goes on and one until, "Hello, this is Nathan, I'm unable to take your call at the moment, but if you-"

"Yeah, I'm sure you can't," I say to myself, clicking the end call button before ringing again.

"Pick up, scumbag." The buzzing sound bounces around in my head, worsening my headache. It doesn't ease when the ringing stops. I tense so hard my head throbs.

One more time. I hit the button and put it to my ear, repeating the words, "Pick up, pick up, pick up," under my breath.

The ringing stops again and I wait for the voice mail, but it never comes. It takes me a second to realise he's answered.

"Hang up on me again and you'll regret it!" I threaten. "I'm giving you the chance to deal with this without consequences." The urge to move hits me again, and I return to my pacing. "Return her and I won't involve the cops, but hang up on me one more time and refuse to give her up, and I'll hand your number over to them."

"She's my daughter," he says, "and I'll protect her from the awful mother she's been forced to live with."

No one has ever hated my mother more than I do, but if he keeps saying these awful things about her as if he knows her, I'm going to lose it.

"You have no idea if she is your daughter or not," I say. "You have no right to take her."

"I have every right."

My hand curls into a fist at my side. "No, you don't!"

"She deserves to-"

I'm sick of it. He's making excuses for himself and none of them are holding up. I don't want to hear anymore from him, I just want him to give me my sister back. So, I cut him off, snarling through the phone. "She deserves to stay with the family she knows."

"She's not happy in your family," he says, softly.

I want to laugh but the anger I'm drowning in prevents that. "And she's happy being kidnapped by a stranger?!"

"I'm not a stranger," I'm told.

How could he honestly think that? He just met her. "To her you are."

He hesitates, filling my ear with silence before replying. "She'll get to know me."

"What if she doesn't want to?" I ask.

"She'll be happier with me," he claims.

Another reason to laugh, but it's suppressed. "How do you know? Have you asked her?"

"I don't need to. She wasn't happy being raised by her mother."

I throw my one free arm up in the air. "How the hell would you know if you didn't ask her?"

"No child would be happy with a mother like Ruth." I hate his calm voice, as if he's talking sense. He's not.

"You know nothing about her, or us!" I shove the small wooden table out of my way as I stumble and bump into it. The legs scrape against the wooden floors, pushing through the debris.

"I know enough."

Trying my best to not scream at the top of my lungs to release my frustration and anger, I push my fingers through my hair, scrunch them up and pull. "I won't tell you again," I seethe, "Bring her back."

"No. She's better off with me."

The blood thrumming in my ears drown out my harsh, rage-filled breaths. I release the tension from my jaw and take a moment to calm my voice. "I want to talk to her."

"I—I don't think so," he says, sounding uncertain.

"Listen here, jackass," I spit at him through my teeth. "Put her on the phone now or I'll find you and shove the phone down your throat."

Beep. Beep. Beep. I'm left in silence until my screams pierce the air.

Calling back proves futile when it doesn't even ring twice before I'm directed to his voicemail. One more time and I want to throw my phone at the wall when I go straight to voicemail without a single ring.

What can I do? What—what do I do? There's no point in ringing. I'll just be wasting more time. So, what do I do now?

Hitting my phone against the side of my head, I push the anger aside momentarily to think back on the Mum's answer.

They could be at the waterpark. Or out to get ice-cream. But she wouldn't—if Misty was somewhere enjoyable, she wouldn't have sounded so scared. Where could they have—Could he have taken her back to his house? How will I know where that is? Where do I start?

I need someone to help me. Or someone to give me more information. How can I—I'll start where I know he's been.

I grab my beanie off the floor and rush out the door. Adrenaline pumps through my veins as I jump into my car and turn the key.

Speeding down the street, I pound my hands on the steering wheel, releasing my frustrations on it.

CHAPTER 9

Pulling up at 'Dale's Pub', I turn my car off and get out, rushing to the entrance.

I scan the inside and find the man behind the bar, pouring a drink for a man in his forties. Pushing past and moving around the other occupants in the pub, I make my way over to him.

I wait for him to finish serving the man and when the man walks away, I open my mouth to speak, but I don't get a sound out before he speaks.

"Hey," he greets me with a smile. "I'm gonna need to see some ID. You look too young to drink."

"I'm not here to drink," I tell him. "Do you know anyone by the name of Nathan? He would have been here last night."

He leans on the bar toward me and widens his smile. "Quite a few people were here last night."

"Well, he would have left with a woman at around five or six in the morning," I explain. "She's 42 but looks like she's 60 while trying to appear 18; with stringy, badly dyed blonde hair. And she wears too much awful coloured makeup. She had on a tight white dress that had a low V neck that was revealing just enough to make you want to stab a fork into your eyes."

He blinks at me, mouth slightly agape. The sounds of the other occupants chatting and enjoying themselves fill the atmosphere. I try to gauge his reaction and thoughts but he gives nothing away.

"Damn, son," he says, standing up straight. "You have a problem with this woman?"

"Yeah, but she's irrelevant," I say. "I'm looking for Nathan. Do you know him?"

He pauses. Crossing his arms and raising his chin, he sizes me up. "Nah. Sorry son. Don't know him."

"Really?" I raise an eyebrow. "'Cause it seems like you do."

"Look." He leans in closer, talking quieter. "Him and his brother have a reputation. They're not people that someone your age should be hanging around."

"I don't want to hang around them. I just want to talk to them."

"Sure you do," he says, rolling his eyes. "I suggest you forget about that stuff, go home, and do whatever homework you have."

It takes me a moment to realise what he's talking about. "I don't—No, I don't want drugs," I tell him. "He took something that doesn't belong to him."

"Ah, got ya. Well, either way." He looks down the bar to the woman waiting to be served. "You should leave them alone and report it to the police. Let them deal with it."

My teeth grind together. "I don't have time to let the cops deal with it. I need to find him now."

"Look pal, I don't have time for this." He speaks through his teeth. "I have customers to serve. Let the cops know he stole your wallet, phone, car, whatever he took, and get out of my bar." With that, he turns and walks over to the woman.

He serves her two clear drinks and when she walks away, I take her place. "Please," I beg.

"Kid, I've had many people in here complaining that he stole something from them. Him and his brother do it all the time." His voice, a low growl, can barley be heard over the constant chatter in the room. "They want me to tell them where to find them, and I tell them what I'm telling you. I can't, and I won't." He picks up a used glass from beside him. "I've contacted the police myself about them, but they've told me they can't do anything about it unless their victims contact them. So, either talk to the police about it or consider whatever he stole gone for good."

He takes the glass and turns away, heading towards a door to the side of the bar.

"He took my sister."

That stops him dead in his tracks. He moves slow, turning back around to face me. Eyes wide. Blinking. Mouth parted. He pinches his brows together. "W—What?"

"My mum brought him home last night," I explain, "and this morning he kidnapped my sister."

"Well, then." He takes slow steps towards me. "You should definitely talk to the police about it."

"Didn't you hear me?" I lean forward, making my voice go as deep as I can. "I don't have time to let the police create an investigation. I need to get her back now."

"You shouldn't be the one going after them."

Who else will? Mum? The police will waste time writing reports. I'm her only hope. "Well, I am. Do you know where to find them or not?"

"I can't give out that type of information," he says.

"Please," I plead. "I won't tell anyone. No one has to know."

"I'm sorry, bud. I really think you should go to the police. Both of them can get a bit aggressive, especially when confronted."

Is that supposed to change my mind?

Pushing myself away from the bar, I say, "All the more reason to get her back as soon as possible."

I don't want to hear anymore from him. He's wasting my time. Time Misty might not have. I'm going to get her back. I give him one last look and strut out the doors.

Halfway to my car, as I unlock it with the button on my key, a voice from behind me catches my attention.

"Hey! Buddy!" I turn to see the barman following after me. He stops in front of me. Concern etched into his features. His stiff demeanour revealing his reluctance. "Honestly, I don't know where he lives...but I've heard he works at Craig's Motors, the auto-repair shop on Fletcher Street." He sighs. "Maybe you could find out more there."

His words pass through my brain like fog through smoke, and it takes time for me to process and understand them.

I had no idea where to go from here. The only plan I had was to drive around, asking people if they knew him, and searching for him and my sister. He just shone a light in the tunnel and pointed me towards towards a possible exit. He's given me hope.

I stutter my words out, pushing past my shock. "Uh- oh- Thanks."

"Good luck," he says, holding his hand out to me, "and stay safe."

Taking his hand, he gives me a strong handshake and I give him a small nod. He turns and walks back towards the pub. I walk the short distance to my car and open the door, but before I can get in I hear him shout from the doorway.

"And don't do anything you'll regret."

With that, he disappears behind the doors and I climb into my car.

Next destination, the repair shop. Good thing I know where it is.

Chapter 10

As I pull up and stop my car at the garage, a mechanic pulls his head out from under the hood of a car and stares at me.

I try to ignore the ill feeling in my gut. Everything about him makes me nervous.

Tangled, dusty blonde hair reaches the middle of his neck, framing his pointed face. The grease on his face—staining his overgrown stubble—doesn't hide his sharp jawline and intense features. Thick eyebrows make his dark, empty eyes more piercing and fierce.

When I get out, he walks towards me, putting a smile on his face that does nothing to make him appear friendly. "What can I do for ya today?" He asks, rubbing his hands on a rag he pulls out of the pocket in his pants.

"I'm looking for Nathan," I tell him. "Is he here?"

"No, sorry," he says, stopping and crossing his arms. "He's out sick."

Sure he is. I'm sure he's so sick he can't even get out of bed. What a load of crap. Sick in the head maybe.

"Do you know where I could find him?" I ask, keeping my voice calm and steady.

He tucks the rag back in his pocket. "Is there anything I can help you with?"

"Yeah, you could tell me where to find him?"

I already hate this guy. He's standing in the way of me finding Nathan and my sister.

"I don't know where he is," he says, not even trying to sound the slightest bit convincing. "But I'm sure I could help you if you tell me what the problem is."

"I need to find him." I do my best to hold my anger at bay. "Do you know his address?"

He hesitates a second, then says, "I don't."

He's lying. It's not hard to tell.

"Give it to me," I demand.

He folds his arms over his chest. "I can't do that." The dirty grey button-up uniform hugs him tight around his biceps and massive shoulders. His bare arms show his suntanned skin, glowing red with recent sunburn.

"Of course you can," I say. "Just write it down, slip it to me, and walk away."

"Maybe you should leave." He takes a step towards me, and although my gut tells me to step back and keep distance between us, I stand my ground.

"I'm not going anywhere until you give me his address."

"I'm not going to do that." He steps forward again. "Leave." He easily passes six foot in height, probably close to six foot five.

"I need to know where he is."

"I don't care." Stepping forward once more puts him in arms length of me and he seizes his opportunity before I have a chance to move, shoving me backwards.

"You should," I say attempting to gain my balance.

"Get out of here, boy." Another shove.

I stumble into the gutter, but I'm saved from crashing to the ground by my car.

He stands there, staring at me, waiting with his arms crossed for me to leave.

I straighten up, move to the side and open the car door. "You better hope he doesn't hurt my sister."

As I'm about to get in the car, he scoffs and asks, "What are you talking about?"

I stop and glare at him. "He kidnapped my little sister this morning."

His arms untangle themselves to fall to his sides, as his sharp stare softens with shock. "He wouldn't do that."

"Well, he did," I spit.

"Nathan isn't that type of person," he says. "I believe you have the wrong man."

"I don't think I do." I step out from behind my car door, letting it shut softy. "He slept with my mum and then left with my sister."

"I know him," he tells me, taking a step. "He wouldn't do something like that."

"Obviously, you don't know him as well as you thought you did."

His body tenses, pushing his shoulders back and puffing out his chest. "I know him better than you."

"Then you should know what an awful piece of crap he is."

Without warning, he closes the gap between us, grabs hold of the front of my black flannel shirt worn over my plain white singlet shirt, and slams me back against the car. "You better watch it! That's my brother you're talking about!"

"He's your brother?" I say, bewildered. That actually makes sense.

"Get the hell out of here before I put your head through your car window." He shoves me back against the car and lets me go.

Once again, he waits for me to follow his orders.

I get into my car and start it up. He doesn't move even as I pull away from the curb, and as I turn the corner, I see him still standing in the same spot, watching me.

When I disappear from his sight, I pull off to the the side, between two other cars and turn my car off. Getting out, I make my up the side of the mechanic shop.

I make it to the corner of the shop and peer around in time to see him on his phone. He puts his phone down on a small wheeled table and puts his head back under the hood of the car. The phone rings as he works on the car.

I pull my head back around the corner, leaning against the wall, and remain hidden as I listen.

The ringing stops and a second later a familiar voice answers. "Hey, Chris."

"Hey," his brother, Chris, replies. "What's going on? What have you done?"

"What are you talking about?" Nathan asks.

"Some kid just turned up asking about you and insisting that you took his sister."

"Shit!" the scumbag says.

I hear the sound of a metal tool of some kind being tossed down on something metal. "So you did kidnap a little girl?"

"Yeah."

"What the hell, Nathan?!" His voice explodes around the shed, making it easy for me to eavesdrop. "You whine every time I make you knock off some car parts or jewellery or some guy's wallet, but you find it just fine to take some random kid?"

"She's mine, bro," he says, testing my resistance to jump out from my hiding place and correct him. She's not his. She doesn't belong with him.

"What are you talking about?" asks Chris.

"She's my daughter. I found out about her this morning."

There's a pause in the conversation, then Chris asks, "How is that possible?"

"You know that chick I dated for a month seven years ago?"

"No," he replies, bluntly.

"The one with the ten year old boy." I can't believe he remembers me, considering he spent zero time with me while he was with Mum.

"Nope." I'm sure he's not giving it any thought. His monotone voice tells me he doesn't care about the story.

"The one you said you loved me dating because it was easy to steal from her."

"No." That has to be a lie. My mother is the easiest person to remember. One meeting with her and she'll be tattooed in your mind for the rest of your life. Her face. He voice. Her terrible personality. No one could ever forget her.

"Well, anyway," he continues. "I ran into her again last night and we went back to her place-"

His brother cuts him off. "Please skip over whatever comes next. I don't need those details."

Neither do I. The last thing I need to know about is more of my mother's sex life.

"She has another kid," he says. "A seven year old " He pauses, but Chris stays silent so he keeps explaining. "And I was the one with her seven years ago...when she would have been conceived."

"Did she directly tell you she's your kid?" Chris asks him.

"No," he answers, "but I did the math and-"

He cuts him off a second time. "You're a bloody idiot?"

"What?" he says, defensively.

"You have no idea if she's your kid or not." His voice echoes around the shed. "And you just took her?"

"What do you mean?" he says, raising his voice, making it easier for me to hear him. "I just told you, I was with her at the time she-" He's cut off again.

"She could have been sleeping with ten other guys at the same time."

That's what I said.

He continues, "You have no idea whose kid she is."

"She's mine," he says, and I have never wanted to punch someone in the face more than right now.

"You're delusional," his brother tells him. I agree. Something is serious wrong with that man's head. "Is she with you right now?" he asks.

I listen closely for his answer. "Yeah."

My blood boils.

"You need to take her back."

Yes! Yes! Bring her back. Listen to your brother.

"I can't do that."

I grind my teeth together and clench my jaw to stop from screaming out.

"Why the hell not?" Chris says, rattling around with more tools.

I peer around the corner, hoping I don't make eye contact with him, and find him still looking at the engine of the car.

"Her mother isn't fit to raise her."

"Listen," Chris says, turning around to grab something off the table.

I duck behind the building, silently cursing to myself, certain he caught me. When he continues, I'm able to relax.

"It doesn't matter if you're her father, kidnap is kidnap and you could be charged for this."

At least one of them has a brain. I hope he's able to talk some sense into him.

"You should hear what she has to deal with," he tells him. "Her mother treats her terribly."

"Who cares?! She's not our responsibility." Thank you, I want to scream. "Take her back, forget that you ever knew her, and get back here and help me."

"No."

"I'm not missing around, Nathan," he growls.

"Neither am I," he replies. "Whether I'm her father or not she deserves someone better than her mother."

I want to hurt him. Who is he to make that decision for someone he just met?

"And you honestly think you could be that for her?"

"Yeah."

No. I close my eyes and take a deep breath, trying to calm myself before I do something I'll regret.

"You can't be serious?"

"I am."

I take another look around the corner, holding my breath and letting go when I spot his back towards me and his head under the hood.

"Nathan, you can barely take care of yourself," Chris says, making each word clear. "There's no way you could raise a child."

"I'll figure it out," he replies.

"For goodness sake!" he says, whipping around, forcing me back behind the building just as fast. "Where the hell are you?"

I push myself against the tin wall, trying to get as close to the corner of the shed as possible without being seen, not caring about the bolts that dig into my shoulders. My heart races loudly in my ears. I hold my breath, afraid any small sound could make me miss the answer.

"Sandcastle," Nathan says, confusing me. I couldn't have heard that right. That doesn't make any sense.

"Alright, stay there. I'm on my way."

What the...? How could I have misheard him? What did he say? He couldn't have said sandcastle. He's not in a- It's a code word!!

Chris walks out of the shed. If he were to turn around or look back right now, he would spot me. I hold my breath as he makes his way to his car.

How will I know where to go if they're using code words?

Before he opens the car door, I get an idea. I bolt back to my car. I get there, but before I have a chance to reach for the handle, his car drives around the corner and I have to duck down behind the line of parked cars so he doesn't see me. As soon as he's driven past, I jump in and follow him.

I keep the distance between him and me so I don't make it obvious to him that he's being followed. I allow other cars to come between us and block my view from him but keep my eyes peeled for his car in case he turns or changes lanes.

While in traffic, there's no doubt it works. However, when we drive out of town and the traffic dwindles down until it's just the two of us on the road, it becomes a little more obvious. It doesn't help that he knows what my car looks like.

I do my best to keep a distance between us so he doesn't notice me, but I can tell when he realises it's me behind him. He speeds up without warning, and I have to do the same to keep up with him.

I'm able to close the distance between us until I'm right up behind him. That's when he slams on the brakes.

I avoid crashing into him by stomping my foot down on my brakes and swerving onto the other side of the road. I'm thankful for the empty stretch of road, with no danger of an accident.

He speeds up again, passing me. I pull back in behind him, refusing to let him to get too far.

We swerve everywhere. On the other side of the road. Off the road. We're all over the place.

After a while, when he swerves off the road, I assume he will swerve back on, and I almost miss the dirt road he pulls onto. I notice it at the last second and make a quick movement to stay behind him.

The bumps throw me around in my seat, only being held in place by my seatbelt. It becomes harder to keep up with him travelling over the rough terrain. At times, my wheels leave the ground before slamming back down again, causing my heart to skip a beat. He seems to drive with ease. He doesn't brake or slow; he travels the road like he's on a rail. I, on the other hand, have to constantly correct myself and slow down at times.

The road stretches on longer than I expect. It just keeps going. I have no idea where we're heading or if we even have a destination. This road could lead to nowhere. Where would we go from there? What would we do if we come to a dead end?

He swerves hard. I only see the ditch as I hit it.

Time slows. The world becomes a blur. My mind goes blank and my heart stops.

I watch everything warp and reel.

A deafening, crushing sound fills my ears, bouncing around in my skull. Only for a second.

Darkness. That's all I know next. I'm surrounded by it. Darkness and silence.

My vision comes back first. It takes me a moment for me to understand why nothing makes sense and I don't know where I am. I'm held in by my seatbelt; the only reason I'm not on my head.

Looking down at the roof of the car, glass sprinkling from my hair into the layer of glass already there. Glancing out the smashed windshield, I catch the last sight of Chris's car driving off into the distance, disappearing over a hill.

The seat belt pulls against my chest, restricting my harsh breaths, and allowing me to feel my racing heartbeat throughout my entire body. It pounds in my head, worsening the headache that I now have.

I whip my head around, trying to figure out what to do, but I only create a dizzy spell for me to go through as well.

More shattered glass showers down as I let go of the steering wheel and reach down to place one hand on the ceiling. The glass shards dig into my palm.

With my other hand, I reach up and feel around until my fingers find the seatbelt clip. I brace myself for the impact, lifting my head, and click the button. I land on the back of my shoulders, the glass cutting through my shirt.

Grunting, I turn myself the right way and pull myself out through the shattered window. Dragging myself over glass and rocks, then I get to my feet, wincing.

I look around. I'm in the middle of nowhere. I'm far out of town and now I have no vehicle to get back. What do I do?

Chapter 11

There's no way I could walk back. It would take me all night to get to the outside of town. I'll have to find another way back.

I'd rather die than call Mum to ask her to pick me up, so that option is is out.

I could call a taxi, but I wouldn't know how to give them my location to find me.

My friends! They can all drive and I'm sure they wouldn't mind giving me a lift.

I scramble back into my car, earning a few more cuts, scrapes, and scratches. My phone sits among the mess and it doesn't take me long to find it.

The once intact screen has been blessed with a large staggering crack from the top left corner heading down toward the bottom right corner. Tiny pieces of glass fall out from the spiderweb shatter in the top corner. I'll have to remember that when I put the phone to my ear.

Thankfully, the screen still turns on and the phone proves to be usable.

On the way out, I spot my grey beanie lying on the roof of the car. I hadn't even realised I wasn't wearing it anymore. I grab it as well as I push myself back out.

Before I can get back out of the car, I already have my phone open and my contacts up. I search for my friends' names and click on the first one that comes up, holding the phone up to my ear.

While it rings, I stretch out my arms, pull my long sleeves back, and check for injuries. From what I can see, there's nothing too serious, just a lot of scratches and small cuts. I'm sure tomorrow I'll also be littered with several bruises.

As I lift up my shirt to check for any serious bleeding under there, the ringing stops and a second later I hear Axel's voice through the phone. "Hey mate," he answers cheerfully. "You still coming to Jonah's house soon? Or are you on your way now?"

Before I can give him an answer, he continues talking. "Wyatt just got here," he tells me as I search my torso, spotting a few spots of blood on my white singlet tee. "I bought some snacks after the game, but you better get here fast if you want some, because Jonah keeps eating them all."

I find a cut situated just above the band of my black sweatpants on my left side.

In the background, I hear Jonah reply. "They're here to eat, so I will."

"Leave some for everyone else," Axel scolds with his smile showing through his voice.

"Nah," Jonah says, sounding like he has a mouth full of food. "Everyone else can starve."

Laughter follows, and in other circumstances, I would join in but I can't right now.

Holding the end of my shirt in my hand, I use my fingers on the same hand to reach down to the cut to check the seriousness of it.

"So, you coming?" Axel asks, "What happened with your mum?"

With my pointer and middle finger, I to pull the skin above the cut up to see how deep it is. Blood pours out and a sharp sting erupts from it. Gritting my teeth and letting go, I groan.

Axel hears it and loses his cheerful tone. "You right, mate?"

Taking a deep breath, I ignore his question and say, "I need you to come get me."

"What happened?" I've never heard him talk with a tone as deadly serious as this.

"My car rolled," I tell him, pulling my shirt down. I'm glad the cut isn't that deep, but it still hurts like hell.

"Shit!" Axel shouts, and the distant conversation between Jonah and Wyatt goes silent. "You okay?"

"Yeah," I lie. "I'm fine. Can you pick me up?"

"Yeah, of course." The ruffling sounds let me know he's already on the move. "I'm on my way right now."

"What happened," someone says in the background. I can't tell right away if it's Jonah or Wyatt, and I can't be bothered to think about it and figure it out.

"Dorian rolled his car," Axel explains, his voice further away from the phone than before.

"Shit!" they both say, almost in unison.

More ruffling about fills the speaker, and amongst it, I catch Axel's frantic words. "Where are my keys?"

After I listen to a couple more seconds of the sound of movement, I hear one of them shout, "They're here!" I hear the sound of keys jingling.

"Get in the car now!" orders Axel. "Lets go!"

The ruffling sound returns and I use the time to run my hands up and down my legs, searching for injuries hidden under my pants. I find several places that hurt, but nothing too bad. I'm sure it's just bruises.

The sound of a car door slamming shut and the engine roaring to life catches my attention. A moment later, the ruffling stops and Axel speaks. "You still there, Dorian?"

"Yeah," I reply.

"We're coming now," he tells me. "Where are you?"

"I don't know."

"Okay, send your location to Wyatt's or Jonah's phone." As I pull the phone away from my ear, he speaks again and I push it back against the side of my face. "But stay on the phone with me."

"Alright," I say. "One sec."

I find maps on my phone and get my location. I press the "share my location" button and send my location to Jonah's phone, and place the phone back on the side of my face while it sends.

"Okay," I say, letting them know it's on the way.

It doesn't take long for Jonah to announce, "Got it!" There's a second of silence, where I imagine Jonah is pulling up the information I gave him, then quietly he says, "What are you doing there?"

I don't get a chance to give him an answer when Wyatt pipes up and asks, "So, what happened?"

I decide not to beat around the bush with it and just tell them straight. "Misty was kidnapped."

Without hesitation, all three of them say, "What?!"

I begin to explain everything while I walk away from my car, heading in the direction I saw Chris drive off towards.

Chapter 12

As I drag my feet down the dirt road, I notice the setting sun, and I hope the boys make it to me before I'm left in the dark.

"Alright, mate," says Axel. "We're five minutes away."

"Okay," I reply.

Realising I'm still walking and I've walked quiet far, I stop, standing in the middle of the road.

"You still doing alright?" he asks me.

"Yeah, I'm good." No, I'm not. My head throbs and every part of me aches. I turn and look back the way I came.

"Are you badly injured?'

"No, I'm fine. Just a few bumps and bruises."

At that exact moment, I notice a tickling sensation trailing down my right cheek, and when I reach up to see what it is, my fingers come in contact with something wet. I pull them away and stare at the red liquid coating the end of my fingers. My hand follows the trail up my face until it hits a spot on my hairline and I flinch away, groaning into the phone at the sudden pain.

"Somehow, I don't believe you," Axel says.

Wyatt, who sounds the furthest away, asks, "Should we call you an ambulance?"

"No," I reply. "I'm fine." I place my fingers back on the wound on my head. "Just get here." I wince at contact, but I don't pull away. My fingers feel around at the lump on my head that stands out like an elephant in a tree. There's no missing it.

"We're coming," says Jonah. "But we can't put your bones back together."

"I don't need you to," I tell him. "I'm fine."

The lump feels massive. I run my fingers around it.

"How many times are you going to tell us you're fine when you're clearly not?" Axel asks and I hear one chuckle from the background, and I assume it's Jonah.

"As many times..." I stupidly push down on the lump with my finger tips, and a strong pain shoots through my skull, forcing a groan out of me. "...as it takes," I continue, leaving the lump alone, "for me to believe it."

Not wanting to be on my feet any longer, I squat down to sit on the ground, groaning the entire way down.

"We're almost there, mate. Just hold on."

"I'm not dying," I say, although it certainly feels like it.

"You sound like you are," Jonah says.

Putting my head in my free hand and leaning my elbow onto my bent knees, I reply, "I'm fine."

Jonah gives me one short laugh but when he talks, his voice holds no joy. "Alright, buddy."

A silence fills the line. While I wait, I put the phone call on speaker and sit my phone on the ground. Slowly, I lower myself back until the rocks on the road dig into my back. I stare up at the darkening sky, watching the few clouds float across, and the several birds that soar above me.

I close my eyes, wanting the ache to stop but I know I won't be able to relax with the rocks in my back.

Their quiet voices come through the phone again. "It says he should be here somewhere."

"Yeah, there's his car."

"Shit! That looks bad."

"Dorian?" Axel says, louder. "You still there?"

"Yeah," I answer without opening my eyes, moving, or grabbing my phone.

"We're here," he says. "Where are you?"

"I walked a little further down," I tell him.

"Why would you do that?" Jonah asks.

"I didn't want the car to kill me if it decided to explode."

"Oh, okay," he replies. "Yeah, that was a good idea."

"Thanks," I say, with no conviction.

"Where are you now though?" asks Axel.

"Up ahead," I tell them. "Just keep driving until you see me." Then under my breath, I say, to quiet for them to hear, "Or hit me. Either will do."

With no voices coming through the phone, it becomes quiet enough to hear the car approaching.

As I hear the rocks crunching under the wheels, coming up the small hill I'm on, Jonah shouts, "There he is!"

"Damn, bro," Wyatt says. "You sure you're good?"

Despite not wanting to move, I sit up. "Yeah." I pick up my phone, hang up, and walk over to the car.

The second I open the car door, Wyatt says, "You look terrible."

"I'm fine," I reply, climbing into the car to sit next to him.

Jonah scoffs and chuckles from the passenger seat.

Axel angles the rear view mirror to look at me in the seat behind him. "Where to now?"

Before I can give him an answer, Wyatt says, "The hospital."

Axel puts the car into gear but I stop him from moving by saying, "No. Keep driving forward."

Both Wyatt and Jonah look at me confused, but Axel follows my orders and drives forward, continuing down the dirt road at a slow pace.

"Where are we going?" he asks, looking in the mirror at me for just a second before directing his eyes back to the road.

"I don't know," I answer. "Wherever Chris went."

Axel stop the car. "Dorian, maybe that's not a good idea."

"Why not?" I say, sitting forward, causing my head to spin for a moment. "He has my sister."

"I think it would be best to let the police deal w th it," Wyatt says, following my movement forward.

"I don't think it would be," I say back. I shoot daggers at him with my eyes. "Chris knew I was following him. He could do something to Misty," I explain. "And we're already closer than the police would be anyway."

"Bro, you need to go to the hospital," Wyatt says to me.

"No. I don't," I tell him. "I need to find my sister."

"Dude," Jonah says, turning around in his seat. "You have blood pouring down your face."

I reach up and wipe the sticky blood off onto my hand. "And who knows what Misty's dealing with at the moment? She could be hurt too."

The image of my little sister, bloody and scared, pops into my head, making my heart sink and my stomach turn.

Axel speaks, ridding my mind of the horrible image. "The police will get her back," he says. "She'll be alright. You need to see a doctor."

"I don't care about me right now." My voice rises. "I'm not going anywhere until I get Misty back."

"I think you should go to the hospital." Wyatt leans back in his chair.

"It doesn't matter what he wants," Axel tells him. "I'm the one driving the car." He drives forward and for a moment I'm sure he's on my side, then he angles himself off the road, heading down the hill, stops, and throws the car in reverse.

My heart races as I watch him turn the car around. "No. Axel, please," I beg, pulling myself against his seat, looking over his shoulder. "We could be so close."

"Or we could be so far away." He drives forward again, stopping at the edge.

"Why does it matter? It's my sister. Please, stop. Turn back around."

He reverses once more. After this he just has to pull forward and we'll be off and gone.

Jonah looks back at me. "Dorian, it's not a good idea to go after these guys. We don't know what they're capable of."

"All the more reason to go after them and get Misty now." I slap the back of the seat with desperation. I've never felt so insignificant and unheard in my life.

"Dorian-" Axels begins.

As he starts to drive forward down the dirt road, I realise I don't have to let them decide. I can take full control of the situation too.

"No," I cut him off. "If you don't want to help, fine, you don't have to, but I'm not leaving Misty." I open the door and with the car still slowly moving, I step out.

"Dorian!" Wyatt cries out. He attempts to grab a hold of me, but I'm already out.

"You guys go back home," I tell them, the car coming to a stop. "Wish me luck."

Before they can reply, I slam the door shut and walk away.

Following the path Chris had gone, I wonder how far I'll have to walk. Will I get there soon, or will I reach the destination sometime tomorrow?

While in thought, the car comes up behind me, but I don't notice it until they honk once.

Wyatt opens the same door I jumped out of, while Axel leans out his open window and sighs, saying, "Get in."

"No." I say, without turning around. "I'm going to find her."

The car follows behind me, barely moving at all.

"We're not leaving you here," he says.

"I'm not leaving Misty," I say over my shoulder.

"We know," he sighs. "We'll help you find them, just get in the car."

I stop walking and turn around. The car stops in front of me. With the sun behind the mountains, I can't see them behind the tinted glass, so I just stare at the spot where I know Axel is sitting.

I don't believe them. I'll get in the car and they'll hold me down, turn back around, and drive off. No way. Not happening.

He sticks his head out the window. "We will," he assures me. "Come on."

I consider it for a second, and decide to trust them. Wyatt scoots over to let me in, and I take my seat beside him. Holding my breath, I wait for the car to start turning around, and I'll jump out before they can get me, but we drive forward instead.

Jonah and Wyatt stare at me as we travel while I try to pretend like they aren't looking at me at all.

I wipe the blood from my face with the under side of my unbuttoned shirt. I know not all of it comes off and I'm sure I'm just spreading most of it around on my face, but I don't care.

Watching me do it, Jonah says, "You're insane, man."

"I'm fine."

"Yeah," Jonah says under his breath, turning back around to stare ahead of him. "So I've heard."

CHAPTER 13

I lean my head back against the headrest, closing my eyes, wishing the aching away.

"What are we looking for?" Axel asks.

"He was driving a black Land Rover ," I tell him, not bothering to open my eyes or lift my head. "Just keep driving and hopefully we'll see it."

"And if we don't?" asks Jonah.

"I don't know." I have no idea. I hadn't thought that far ahead and I can't control my mind at the moment to come up with an answer.

We drive in silence. No one talks to me and I become so lost in thought that if they did, I'm certain I wouldn't hear them.

I hope we find her, I think. I hope she's okay. I can't imagine how scared she would have been while he was chasing her around the house. Chasing her—trying to take her when clearly didn't—she—clearly she didn't want to go. How scared is she—she would be terrified. Scared out of her mind. I have to get to her. She'd be so scared. What would they do to her? Hurt—would they—would they hurt her?

If they hurt her, I'll—I swear, I'll make them swallow their teeth.

We have to find her. We have to. But...if we don't? Do we—What do we do then? I could call the cops. Am I too late. Should I have called them back at the house? I told Mum to call them, so should—why didn't I call them?

If by the time the police—if they—if by the time I tell the police. What if they get away? They could—What if they hurt her—kill—hurt her—hurt her because he kno—I'm here. Would the police be better? Would they find her—ever—in time?

They might—we—if—r ever find her.

Could she—would escape. Make a run for it. They could easily catch her—easy. Then what? Would they—Would they?

What's their plan?! If Chris doesn't want her, will he let her go? Bring her—Will he get rid of her, and the evidence? I have to get to her.

I place my elbows on my knees and my head in my hands. With a groan and a sigh, I say, "What if we don't find her?"

"We will, mate," Axel reassures me, changing his tune.

"She'll be alright," Jonah follows along, despite his doubt beforehand.

I pull the beanie off my head and throw it on the empty seat between Wyatt and I. My fingers run through my hair, tugging the clumps in my grip, ignoring and enjoying the pain. "What if we're too late?"

"You can't think like that, mate," Axel says to me.

"You said he took her because he believes he's her father," he says, "and wants to raise her better than your mother, so most likely he won't hurt her."

He's right, I think. It makes sense. He wanted to take care of her so that should be what he does. But—Chris—

"I just don't know what to do," I say, sitting up. "I don't know how to deal with it all."

"That's because your not the adult," Wyatt says. "You mother should be the one dealing with all this."

"She couldn't care less," I say, looking out my window. "It's was almost like she was glad she was gone. Like she didn't have to take care of her anymore or organise her life around her child." The familiar ache of neglect hits my heart, and like every other time, I push it away and refuse to let it take over. "To her," I continue, "Misty and I are just a ball and chain around her ankle, keeping her from doing everything she wants to do. So, Misty going missing would be a blessing for her." The only thing she hates now is me.

She's probably hoping that I don't come back from this either. I won't. Whether I have Misty with me or not, I will not return to her house again. Even if I have to live in a box on the street, I'm never going back.

A silence fills the car. I resort back to pulling at my hair, trying to stop the turmoil in my head from creating a tornado.

"I'm telling ya," I begin, "if I find Misty-"

"When we find Misty," Wyatt cuts me off, correcting me.

"Right," I agree, not truly believing it. "When we find Misty," I continue, "I'm not letting her go back to our mother." I don't care if Misty hates me for it, I'm moving out, and I'm taking her with me.

"What about the money situation?" asks Axel.

"Yeah," Jonah agrees. "You were trying to save up enough to support yourself, if you take Misty, that's another person you have to support."

"What am I supposed to do?" I say, ripping my hands from my messy hair. "Leave her with the heartless beast."

"That was your plan," Jonah states.

"I know," I say, "but plans change. Now I know Mum can't even be trusted to put up with her. I doubt mum would have even fought for her if she came home and saw him trying to take her. She probably would have shoved her into his arms."

None of them disagree with me. We're back in silence.

I hate the silence. It gives me a reason to think about everything. Going over every option and possibility. Everything that went wrong. How it could have been prevented. Why I'm not innocent in this.

I give a long groan. "I shouldn't have left this morning."

"You can't blame yourself for this," Axel tells me.

"Mum told me not to leave because I had to look after Misty. I should have known Mum isn't responsible enough to look after anyone."

"You couldn't have known this would happen," Jonah says.

"Yeah," says Wyatt. "You couldn't have predicted your mum would leave her alone with a stranger."

"Yes, I could," I say, my heart becoming heavier with each moment that passes. "I know my mum. She's done worse."

"You can't blame yourself for this," Wyatt says, underestimating my self-loathing skills.

Axel looks at me using the rear-view mirror. "At least you care enough to do something about it."

"If I had-" I begin.

"Listen here, you little shit," Jonah says, shifting in his seat, turning around to look at me, jabbing a finger at me. "You are not the cause of this. Your mother is to blame."

I stare at him, trying to take in his words but finding it difficult with the shock of his sudden outburst.

"Misty is her child," he continues, "and her responsibility, and she should have taken better care of her. But she left her in the hands of some random. She did this. Not you. You got it?!"

"Yeah," I reply.

"Good." He turns back around, looking out at the front.

I can't help the slight smile that forces its way onto my face. I can't believe that tough-love speech actually worked.

"I think you could have been a little more sensitive," Axel says to him.

"Nah," Jonah replies. "He needed harsh."

My smile stretches bigger. "Thanks," I say in a quiet voice.

While I look out my window, I hear Jonah chuckle. "No problem, buddy."

We go back to silence. Which means, I'm left alone with my thoughts again.

Mum is a horrible person. Awful. I can't stand to be near her anymore. But I would rather Misty be with Mum right now rather than with the two men that have her. At least with Mum I know the worst that could happen would be her being neglected—or I had thought. But better her—I'd rather her than Nathan and Chris.

Nathan might want to take care of her—Chris doesn't seem—doesn't want her. How will Chris deal with—kill—could Nathan protect her from—would he? Would he give in? Let Chris control the situation? How will he fix it? Change—deal with it? Is Misty—she—Can I get—Will I be able—what if—

I return to tugging at my hair.

"Dorian," says Wyatt, noticing my current horrible habit. "You need to stop worrying about it all."

Something inside of me snaps. "How the hell am I supposed to that?!" I whip my head around to face him, ignoring the dizziness.

His face falls and he pulls back away from me.

"She could be hurt, or dying! I'm her only hope right now! And I should just give up on her?!"

"Woah," Jonah says, turning around with his hand out to me. "He wasn't saying that." I knew that, but I couldn't stop myself. "He just means you shouldn't torture yourself by wondering about possibilities."

"But they're possibilities," I explain. "They could all be happening."

"And none of them could be happening," he replies.

He's got a point.

"There's no point in wondering right now," Wyatt says, cautiously. "Just focus on getting her back and what you plan on doing to the scum that took her."

They're right. I shouldn't waste my time on panicking about what ifs.

I sit back, entering my head again, changing the path of my thoughts.

I'm going to put their head through whatever wall I can find. I don't care if they're bigger than me, it's four against two. If they hurt her, I'll make sure they regret it. I'll break their kneecaps and force their to rib cage to cave in. I'll-

"There!" Jonah shouts, breaking me from my thoughts and causing me to give a small jump.

Sitting up, I lean into the centre with Wyatt to look out the front and see a house coming into view. My heart races and adrenaline surges through my body at the sight of it. As we drive up to it, I can't sit still. I lift myself out of my seat and drop back down multiple times wanting to be at the house already.

We pull up to the front of the house. I open the door and jump out of the car before it's come to a stop.

Ignoring the three of them calling out to me in harsh whispers, I run up the several long steps and into the already open door.

I run from room to room, searching every hiding space Misty could fit. Cupboards. Under beds. Behind curtains.

Upstairs, I find the master bedroom. During a quick search, I discover one of Misty's toys under the bed. A pink plastic unicorn with rainbow hair.

With my heart trying to break out of my chest, I search the entire room and then do it again. When I come up empty the second time round, I rush out of the bedroom to continue my search elsewhere.

Before I can run into the next room, the room further down catches my attention. I approach the bathroom, staring at the busted door. A sense of déjà vu washes over me, taking me back to our bathroom.

She's made a habit of finding the bathroom to lock herself in to escape. However, both times have failed her.

I don't have to step into the bathroom to know it's a complete mess. Worse than the bathroom at home.

My heart stops as I step in the doorway and look to the side. I'm frozen to the floor, my gaze stuck staring at the red puddle on the tiled floor. I could tell myself it's not hers, if it weren't for her stuffed toy rabbit lying next to it, blood covering its head.

Chapter 14

The world around me crumbles. I pick the rabbit off the floor, and stand frozen, staring at the faded, worn toy.

A tightening in my chest threatens to suffocate me as my heart pounds against it.

I scrunch the rabbit up in my hands, restricting my rage from tearing the head off.

Instead, I snatch the ceramic hand soap pump out of the sink bowl and throw it hard at the wall while letting out a deafening scream. Shards of ceramics fly everywhere. Some stick to the wall, sliding down with the green coloured soap splattered against the white tiles.

With my hands and the rabbit pushed against my face, I listen to the three sets of footsteps running towards me.

I pace the small bathroom until a pair of hands gently pull me to a stop, and I'm led over to the edge of the bathtub and forced to sit down.

My friends, stood around me, don't notice the blood to begin with.

Axel spots it first. He doesn't say anything about it, he just tries to discreetly nudge Jonah's arm to point it out to him. Wyatt follows their gazes and becomes the final one to be clued in with the worse possible piece of evidence.

Turning back, Wyatt places a hand on my shoulder and says, "We don't know if it's hers."

I push off the edge of the bath to get to my feet but Wyatt holds me down. "Whose else's could it be?" I growl up at him.

"It could be their's," Jonah suggests.

"Yeah," Axel agrees. "She might have gotten them."

"Then, where is she?" I ask, rising to my feet despite Wyatt's attempt to hold me down. "What did they do to her?"

"We don't know," answers Axel. "But we'll find her, mate?"

What if we're already too late? That blood could be hers. What if now we're only able to find her body?

"Stop," Jonah says, pulling me from my thoughts.

I look at him, giving him a arched brow. "What?" I didn't do anything.

"I can hear those negative thoughts rolling around in your head," he tells me. "Don't do it to yourself."

"Okay. So, they couldn't have turned back," says Axel, "or we would have seen them, and the car we were looking for isn't here, which means they would have driven further out."

Jonah throws his hands up. "What the hell would be out there?"

"I don't know," Axel replies. "Couldn't be much. I never knew anything was out here."

"Yeah," Wyatt agrees. "I wouldn't have thought a house would be out here."

"Then where could they have gone?" Jonah asks.

"To bury her body where no one will find it," I say under my breath.

Jonah reaches out and slaps me over the head.

"Ow."

"Well, are we going to sit here talking about it," Wyatt says, "or are we going to find them?"

"Good point." Axel agrees. "Let's go." He turns and walks out the door.

Jonah follows him without a word. A single pat on my back from Wyatt encourages me to move and follow them out with Wyatt on my heels.

We make our way through the house to the open door and the car that's still running. Without thinking, we all take the seats we were sitting in before.

I toss the old toy rabbit on the seat with my grey beanie as Axel reverses the car. Silence fills the space between us all. Listening to the tires travelling over the rocks and grave., I lean my head back against the headrest, doing my best to keep the image of my sister's lifeless body out of my head.

Chapter 15

I hadn't noticed the last sight of the setting sun when I came running out of the house. It wasn't until Axel flicked on his headlights that I realised how dark it had become.

The silence deafens me. I wish someone would say something but I can't bring myself to open up my mouth and start a conversation.

Growing tired of looking out the front window at the deserted area, I lean back and close my eyes for a while.

When I open them again, I'm shocked to see the road lined with a thick layer of towering trees on either side.

As the dirt road roughens and we realise Axel, the daredevil, won't slow, we all put our seatbelts on just so we can stay in our seats for a second. The road winds and bends through the woodland area, tossing us around and giving me pain to focus on rather than the thoughts in my head.

The car roars up a hill and as it reaches the top, another car comes into view.

Axel slams on the brakes. "Shit!" he exclaims.

We all fly forward, saved by our seatbelts, and the car comes to a stop behind the almost invisible black car with a hair width gap between the two of them.

"Woah!" Jonah says, staring ahead at it.

"That came out of nowhere." Wyatt holds Jonah's seat in front of him.

Without hesitation, I unclip my seatbelt and throw myself out of the car, running up to the parked car ahead. My hand tugs on the first door handle I get to but I only get a thud from it as it remains closed. I get the same result from the driver's door. I don't bother running around to the other side to check, I assume all the doors are locked. Instead, I hit the hood of the car with my hand and give an anger infused shout.

I peer into the window, using both my hands to see past my reflection, only to be staring at the empty front seats.

A quick glance into the back seats stops my heart. The shadows hide it well, but with the help of the last of the sunlight, I can make out the dark stain on the seat.

The three others walk towards me, showing no interest in the inside of the car. I'm sure my fallen expression has given them the answer they need.

"Where could they have gone now?" Jonah asks calmly, oblivious to the sinking heart I have in my chest.

"The only place they could have gone," Wyatt replies. "In."

Swallowing hard and taking a deep breath in, I'm able to get my words out. "And that's where I'm going."

"Not alone," Jonah says, stepping forward.

"We'll split into pairs." Axel gestures to each of us. "Jonah, you go with Dorian. Wyatt, you're with me."

We walk in together but drift apart to take different paths.

As soon as Axel and Wyatt have vanished into the shadows, I say, "How will we find them out here? They could be anywhere."

The moment of hesitation takes away any reassurance he could try to give me. "I don't know," he answers, discouraging me more.

"Well, thanks for being honest," I say.

"We'll find them," he says, his voice holding no conviction.

"Go back to being honest."

He doesn't reply and we walk in silence. The sounds of sticks snapping beneath our feet echo through the forest.

They would be able to hear us from a mile away. We'll never catch them.

A shout echoes through the trees from my left, and Jonah and I pull to a stop. Footsteps move towards the cars. Jonah and I share a look before we turn and run, following the rushed steps.

Chapter 16

While we sprint towards the cars, we hear Axel and Wyatt calling our names. Neither of us bother to respond. We focus on zig-zagging around the trees and running as fast as we can.

It's difficult to tell if we're getting closer to them or not with my heartbeat pounding in my ears and sticks snapping beneath my shoes.

That doesn't matter though. I'll run until my legs fall off if I have to, no matter how far they get. I have no idea if Jonah has kept up with me or if I left him behind long ago, but I'm not going to slow or even check behind me.

Movement in the shadows and between the flickering sight of the trees catches my eye. I adjust my course slightly to head towards the running figure to my right.

As I get closer to them, I'm able to recognise the figure as Axel. He zips around the trees, his focus ahead of him. I take a quick glance around for Wyatt but I can't spot him. I assume him to be further ahead. Hopefully his athletic skills enable him to catch them both.

He's played multiple sports since grade three, and fell in love with anything that allows him to run. We've helped him train for marathons and races for years. I know fast he can run. I'm sure Nathan and Chris couldn't run faster than him.

As the clearing where our cars are parked comes into view, I'm able to see Wyatt, Chris, and—I assume—Nathan running in an uneven line. I'm happy to see Wyatt has caught up with them, but he's not quite on their heels yet.

Nathan and Chris separate as they reach the car. Chris chooses the driver's seat and Nathan takes the passenger side. My heart sinks as I realise there should be three of them. What did they do with Misty?

I hear the car roar to life from a distance and I'm thankful that Wyatt reaches them before they can move. He runs for Chris's door and pulls on the door handle, but finds it locked. Refusing to give up, he hits the window with his hand and yanks on the handle as the car starts to move.

His athletic ability has allowed him to reach the car before they leave, but it also means he's on his own while we catch up.

Through the windscreen, with the help of the disappearing sunlight and the arising moonlight, I can see Chris becoming frustrated as Wyatt proves that no matter what he won't quit. But what will he do if he gets the door open?

Wyatt blocks Chris's vision as he tries to turn, and causes the car to almost hit a tree. Fuming, Chris swings open the door fast, hitting Wyatt's head and knocking him backwards. He gets out of the parked car, delivering a punch to Wyatt's head. Then, he pulls him up and throws him into the backseat of his car.

All three of us scream at him but he ignores us and gets back into the front seat. He pulls back and turns, ready to drive away, and all we can do is watch.

Axel makes it to the car just in time to hit the back of it once before it speeds away. A scream of frustration explodes through the atmosphere as Axel continues after the car that spits dust up at him.

Before the car disappears over the hill, Axel turns to look back at us still running towards him. With no where to go now, Jonah and I begin to slow our run.

"Hurry up," Axel shouts, rushing back towards us. "Get in the car."

I understand Wyatt could be in trouble, but I can't help but think of Misty. Where is she? Is she okay? They left without her. She must still be here somewhere. I can't leave her.

Jonah passes me as I pull up to a stop. Axel throws open the driver's side door and glances back at us once more.

"You two go get him," I say. "Come back and pick me up once you do."

I see Jonah look back at me before I spin around and run back into the woodland. I hear the two of them calling out to me, but I ignore them and keep running.

Weaving through the forest, I call out to Misty, over and over and over.

She could be anywhere. How on earth will I find her?

I continue to scream her name. What more could I do? What if she can't hear me, or she can't respond? She could be unconscious. God, I hope not. I swear, if they've hurt her, I'll kill 'em.

I'm so focused on running faster and scanning for Misty that I almost miss it.

CHAPTER 17

I slow to a stop. The blue jewellery box I knew to be missing from her bedroom lies in front of me at my feet. On its side with the lid open to show me the empty inside. A red stain covers the top side of the box. My heart pounds.

Further ahead, I see her barbie doll, a bright yellow dinosaur, a pink plastic tea cup, the blue toy car I use to own as a kid, and a stuffed princess doll. All smeared with blood.

I step through them. Moving around them. Making my way forward. I stare at every toy that I pass, finding more the further I go. Pieces of jewellery, wooden blocks, marbles, and painted rocks. The second last thing I come across is a travel bag from Mum's cupboard. Then, I find her coat.

A light brown coat with fluffy fuzz on all the edges. Blood stains the inside and outside.

My fingers come off red as I pick it up and hold it in my hands, staring at it. What did they do to her?

Behind me, I hear running footsteps approaching me. I don't bother to check who it is, knowing it can only be Axel or Jonah.

It turns out to be both. I hear them still calling out to me, but they stop when they spot me.

"I told you to get Wyatt," I say without turning to face them, when I know they're close enough to hear me.

"We're not going to leave you out here," Jonah replies, out of breath.

"What about Wyatt?" I ask, still staring at the coat.

"We'll go get him right now." Jonah slaps his hand down on my shoulder. "Come on."

I scrunch the coat up in my fists. "I can't leave her here," I tell him. "Wherever she is." She could be hurt. She might need help. I can't just walk away and leave her to fend for herself. Not again.

"We'll come back and find her after," Axel says.

She's dead. That's what I hear him trying to tell me. I can here it in his voice. There's no rush in finding her.

"Why would he do this?" I say, talking to no one in particular. "He said he would look after her because he's her father. In what way is this looking after her?"

I receive silence from the two standing behind me.

"She didn't deserve any of this."

Jonah's hand falls from my shoulder.

"They hurt her." My eyes begin to water and I try my hardest to force the moisture away before Axel and Jonah can see it. "They probably killed her." I tighten my grip on the coat and sharpen my expression. Throwing the coat on the ground, I turn and say, "Now, I'll kill them."

Before Axel and Jonah can reply, I storm pass them. I hear them both chase after me. I don't slow down. I won't.

"Dorian!" Jonah calls out. "Wait up." They rush after me, unable to catch up.

When I spot Axel's car in the distance, I shout over my shoulder. "Give me the keys, Axel!"

"I don't think you should drive," he tells me.

"I don't care," I reply, clenching my jaw. "Hand 'em over!" Reaching the car, I turn to look at them, holding my hand out in front of me.

"Not happening," he says, coming to a stop in front of me. "Get in the back."

Anger surging through me, I grab the front of his shirt, spin him around, and slam his back into the side of the car. "Keys! Now!"

"You can beat me up if you want." He remains calm despite my relentless grip. "I'm not letting you get behind the wheel like this."

"Look at what happened the last time you were behind the wheel," Jonah says under his breath. I look over my shoulder to glare at him.

"We're going to get Wyatt back," Axel says, "find your sister, and then leave."

"No," I shout, pushing him back against the car door, "I'm gonna kill them both and-"

He cuts me off with a quiet, calm voice. "We won't let you."

"You can't stop me."

"There's two of us and one of you," he tells me. His refusal to fight back irks me. He keeps his arms by his sides and his body relaxed.

"They deserve it."

"I know they do," he agrees, "but you don't. You'll regret it."

"No, I won't. I'll-"

I'm cut off again. "You will. They'll be dead, but you'll be the one to suffer for the rest of your life."

I want to disagree with him, but a part of me knows he's telling the truth. So, I stay quiet.

"You'll lay awake at night," Axel continues, "repeating that moment over and over in your head."

My grip begins to loosen, allowing him to straighten up a little.

"It'll torture you."

Still, I can't find anything to say.

"Misty won't want you to-"

I don't let him finish. My grip regains it's strength on his shirt and he gets pushed back against the car with a thud. A gasp forces its way past his lips. "Misty was seven!" I scream into his face. "All she wanted was to grow up, an they took that away from her!" Spit flies from my mouth.

With a short pause, he says, "You don't know if she's dead."

Of course she's dead. "Why else would they leave without her." My own words place an ache on my heart.

I can see him wracking his brain for an answer but he comes up with nothing. So, he stays quiet.

With nothing else for me to say, the silence stretches between us.

Breaking that silence, Axel speaks in a voice so quiet, I wouldn't be surprised if Jonah can't hear what he says. "We need to get Wyatt back. Hop in the back and let's go get him."

I hesitate, holding onto him.

Jonah places his hand on my shoulder. "Come on, bud."

Slowly, I release him from my hold. He steps to the side and opens the back door, waiting for me to step inside. Once I'm in, he slams the door shut and gets in his door, and Jonah runs around to get in the passenger seat.

As the car revs to life and starts moving, I focus on keeping the tears at bay.

In the silence, I stare down at the old stuffed rabbit on the seat next to me, sat on top of my grey beanie.

My chest aches as I imagine her happy face framed by her dark blonde hair. Her cheerful and fun loving personality shining through her bright eyes. She had an innocent soul with a pure heart that I always let her know I hated, but secretly, I was jealous. I was jealous she was able to hold onto that part of herself even after everything she had to go through.

She kept her trusting, bubbly nature alive inside her double-sized heart. No one could ever ruin it for her. Not even Mum.

However, Mum's not the only one to blame. I hurt her just as much. But she never let me or Mum stop her from loving life. No matter how much we pushed her to the side, she never let us go.

She always wore a smile every moment of the day. I wouldn't be surprised if she had a smile on her face while she slept at night. Not anymore. I'll never get to appreciate that smile. She'll never get to feel the love she deserves.

I think about the last thing I said to her. I screamed at her to get out after she told me she wanted to stay with me because of a bad dream she had. That bad dream was probably about the hate and ignorance she got from me and Mum.

I always told myself I didn't want to end up like my mum and that's exactly what I became. I'm just as heartless and awful as she is. I turned out just like her. My worst nightmare.

I let this happen. If I had cared a little more about her and took better care of her, this wouldn't have happened. I've been blaming everyone else for this when I'm the one to blame. Mum told me to stay to look after her, and I didn't. I left. I left her. I didn't care and so I left, and that's why she's gone now.

She wanted love and never received it, now she never will, all because of me.

CHAPTER 18

'm going to kill them, I think. I don't care what Axel, Jonah, or Wyatt try to do. I will kill them.

The car drives up to the house, parking next to the black car. Before we come to a stop, I jump out, leaving the door open, running up to the house.

They don't deserve to live. I'm going to cut their throats out and shove them up their nostrils.

I burst through the door and rush into the room without stopping to figure out where I should go first. I'm forced to stop when the man I assumed to be Nathan, walks out of a room off to the side and stops in front of me when he sees me.

I can only see resemblance to Chris in the intense hazel eyes, prominent jaw, and the tall stance. But that's it. Nathan has short brown hair that only covers the top of his ears. Short stubble covers his square face. He has a thin build with pale skin and average defined muscles. I would guess he stands at six foot even, and Chris is definitely taller.

We stare at each other, my body filling with white-hot rage.

"And who are you?" he asks, standing taller.

I don't give him an answer. Instead, I stomp towards him, quickly closing the distance that stands between us.

Before I can reach him, Chris flies out of the same room and gets to me first. A knife hits my neck, and he yanks my arm behind my back hard. My heart flutters with panic.

"This," Chris says, pushing the knife up under my chin, forcing me to lift my head, "is the brother."

"Oh," Nathan says, arching his brow. "I thought you said you-." He does his best to keep his voice calm and strong, but he can't help the slight shake at the end revealing his nerves. I notice the red smears on the front of his light blue shirt and the dark stains on the long sleeves, but I can't see any sign of injury. Not even a strained expression or a strange stance, proving a hidden injury.

So, who's blood is it? And where is Misty?

The room tilts and sways, and if Chris weren't holding me up, I'm sure I'd be on the floor.

Chris cuts him off. "Yeah. I know what I said." He speak to me over my shoulder. "I don't understand how you survived that car roll. But, welcome to the party nonetheless."

At that moment, Axel and Jonah run through the door, their footsteps stopping as they near the doorway.

Chris turns to the side to look at them, allowing me to see them from the corner of my eye. They stand in the doorway, their eyes wide.

"Ahh, there's the other one," Chris says, loud and excited, "and he's brought another friend."

My stomach twists into a tight knot.

"Please," he says, pushing the knife further against my throat. "Come in. The more the merrier."

They make no indication of moving.

"I said," he growls, "come in."

They follow his orders, taking slow steps inside.

"Stand against that wall."

A moment later, I see Jonah and Axel shuffle against the wall in front of me.

"Is this really a good idea, Chris?" Nathan asks in a quiet voice.

"You started this!" Chris's booming voice next to my head makes my ear ring. "I'm just cleaning up your mess."

"This isn't what I wanted," he replies, quieter than before.

"But it's what you've gotten." The knife moves away from my neck for just a second while he gestures to the room they both came out of. "Get in there." As quick as it's removed from my throat, it returns, leaving no time to react in anyway.

Axel and Jonah side step towards the room, never taking their eyes away from me.

Nathan follows them in. Then, with my arm still restrained behind me and the knife pushed into my skin, I forced to walk forward.

I can't help the short intake of breath as I step inside and see Wyatt sat on the floor, tape over his mouth, both hands tied behind his back with rope, and a trail of blood down his face. His wide eyes flick between all of us, his hands tugging on the rope attached to a thick metal loop on the wall.

A long heavy-looking wooden desk sits off to the side of him. Its strange placement tells me they shoved it away from the wall to get to the six hoops hidden by it.

Several tall cupboards line the wall to the right. A couple of the doors stand open, but not enough to see inside. I'm sure they stand against the window, blocking any moonlight from entering. So the only light comes from the dim ceiling light that may as well not be on.

"Stand there," Chris says, gesturing to the right with his elbow, causing the blade to scrape my skin and giving me a reason to flinch.

They do as they're told, standing to the side of the desk.

"Don't move," he tells them. "If either of you move, I'll slit his throat." He pushes the cold blade of the knife harder against my neck. Each time the knife gives a slight twitch, my heart stops.

Both of them stand against the wall of cupboards, flicking me nervous and concerned glances. Jonah fidgets with his fingers in front of him.

"What are you waiting for?!" He shouts into my ear.

Nathan gives a short jump before he turns and hurries away, moving behind us and out of my sight.

I hear him open a cupboard or something and rummage through it. He returns with a roll of tape and rope, and walks over to Wyatt.

"Hurry up!" He's told and his pace quickens.

Nathan gestures for Jonah to walk over to him and stand next to Wyatt.

Jonah stays standing next to Axel, glancing around the room at each of us.

"He said, move!"

I flinch again.

Slowly, Jonah makes his way over to Nathan where he's then told to turn around. His hands are bound with the rope and it's pulled tight to make him wince.

Spun around, he looks to Axel, then to me and Chris. "What are you going to do to us?" he asks, keeping his voice steady.

"Shut up!" Chris shouts, jerking the knife, making me flinch.

"You know if you kill us here," Jonah says, as Nathan pushes him down to his knees, "you'll get blood everywhere. It'll be impossible to get it out."

"I said, shut up." Another jerk. Another flinch.

"We're not going to kill you." Nathan looks back at Chris. "We won't kill them."

"Keep tying" he replies.

"I agree with him," Jonah says, gesturing with his head to Nathan.

Chris's hold on my arm tightens, his nails digg ng in. "Shut up!"

"It's two against one. Majority rules," Jonah continues. I'm not sure it's a good idea to pester him, but he doesn't meet my eye line. He keeps his gaze attached to the one behind me.

Nathan pulls on the rope and ties it to the hoop next to Wyatt. What are they going to do to us?

"Hurry up and tape his mouth," says Chris. "I'm sick of listening to him."

He rips a piece of tape from the roll and sticks it over his mouth.

"Great," Chris says, turning to Axel. "Now for-"

As we turn towards Axel, I see nothing but cupboards lining the wall where he once stood. I move from side to side as Chris looks around the room. Between my quick movements, I catch a glimpse of Jonah and spot the crinkles by his eyes, revealing the smile behind the tape. Realisation strikes me, and I have to try keep the smile off my own face. I can't believe Jonah's distraction workec, and on me too.

"Where is he?!" Chris screams into my ear making it ring.

"He must have snuck out," suggests Nathan.

"Well," he shouts, "find him!"

And just like that, Nathan scurries out of the room.

Chapter 19

I stand here, terrified that Chris will hold up his end of the deal and will slit my throat if Nathan doesn't return with Axel soon enough.

After a minute or two of Chris was shifting on his feet, he barges forward towards Jonah and Wyatt. The knife presses into my neck until we reach the wall, where I'm released. I'm propelled into the wall and when I turn around, I come face to face with the end of the knife.

"Don't move," I'm warned. He kneels and picks up the rope from the floor, still holding the knife out in front of him. Straightening up, he whirls the knife around. "Turn around," he orders.

I do as I'm told, turning to face the wall. Moments later, both my arms get ripped back behind me and the rope snakes around my wrists. It's pulled tight, pinching my skin, and tugged down to force me to the floor. I'm tied to the ring next to Jonah before a piece of tape gets slapped over my mouth.

As soon as he's sure I'm secure and there's no chance of me escaping, he storms out of the room, following his brother in the hunt for Axel.

I stare at the empty door way and into the darkness of the house, hoping Axel isn't found and wondering what will happen if he is.

Movement to the left of the doorway catches my eye and I look over to see the door to a large cupboard opening slowly.

Axel's head peeps out from the inside. I can feel my racing heart thumping hard in my chest.

He rushes over to Wyatt and begins to untie him. My eyes flick back and forth between them and the doorway, panicking that the psycho brothers will walk in.

Wyatt removes the tape from his mouth as soon as his hands are free.

"You good, mate?" Axel asks in a soft whisper.

Wyatt nods, rubbing his wrists, and Axels moves onto Jonah.

Just as Wyatt reaches for my hands, footsteps echoing around the house grow louder and louder.

"How is this my fault?" I hear Nathan say.

"You should have watched him." Chris replies.

I use my head to indicate for them to leave us and go.

They both dash away and Axel hides in the same cupboard and Wyatt finds a place to hide in another.

"I was tying the boy up," Nathan says, "you should have been watching the other one."

"You're the reason why we're in this mess in the first place," blames Chris. "Everything's your fault."

They both step through the wide doorway, pointing fingers at each other.

"You're the one that-"

Chris cuts him off when he notices one of us missing. Stopping in the doorway, Nathan stopping beside him, his eyes widen and his nostrils flare. "Where did the black one go?!" he shouts.

Nathan clears his throat. "I think that's racist," he says in a soft and quiet voice.

Chris turns to his brother, his face glowing red. "Does it look like I care?!" He storms over to Jonah and I. Grabbing the front of my shirt, he yanks me up to my knees and leans down until our noses touch. "Where did they go?!" he screams, spit hitting my face, his eyes wide and wild.

While still holding onto me, he reaches down and pulls Jonah up too, forcing him onto his knees, the rope tied to the hoop pulled tight like mine. "Tell me now!"

I don't know how he expects us to answer with tape over our mouths. Head guestures?

After getting nothing from us, he throws us back down to the floor.

"What do we do?" says Nathan, nervous and unsure.

Chris cracks every knuckle possible on his hands in two swift movements and storms over to Nathan. Without hesitation, his hand flies back and swings to hit his brother hard on the cheek. "Find them!"

Nathan holds his face in his hands. Disbelief fills his eyes.

"They're here somewhere!" Chris stands over Nathan, getting as close to him as possible. "Get them!"

Nathan shrinks back and speaks in a quiet voice. "How?" He removes his hand from his cheek that glows red. As soon as he does it, I know he's made a big mistake.

Chris changes his tone to talk in a soft yet sharp voice. "Hmm," he says, faking a thinking process. "How about you try..." He drops his fingers from his chin, balls both hands into fists and screams, "...using your eyes!"

"Where do I start?" he asks, flinching back, clearly expecting another hit.

He should have prepared better for the hit, although I feel like nothing would have stopped Chris from delivering the powerful hit to the side of his head.

"Use that tiny brain you have, and think! They have to be in this room somewhere."

Nathan doesn't move, instead he rubs his hand over the contact point of the hit. Honestly, he deserves the hits he gets if he can't realise everything he's doing wrong.

"Start searching!"

He looks around the room and picks a place to start his search.

Chris stands back and watches him, waiting for him to do all the work and find them.

Nathan makes his way around the room, searching every hiding spot as he goes. Nerves swirls around in my stomach the closer he gets to the cupboards where Axel and Wyatt hide. I'm glad he appears to be taking his time, but he'll get to them eventually and when he does, we're all screwed.

Only steps away from the hiding spot, Chris says, "This is taking too long." He turns to face me and Jonah, stalking towards us. "Let's speed things up."

Thanks to his brother's impatience, Nathan stops his search, standing in front of Axel's cupboard, and watches him approach us.

He bends down, unties the rope connecting Jonah to the hoop, leaving the second piece of rope used to bound his hands, and pulls him to his feet. Dragging him to the centre of the room, he says, "Come out now and I won't hurt your friend."

Yeah, and as soon as they do, you'll kill us all.

He waits for them to come out and I hope they don't give in that easy. When nothing happens, he sends his fist into Jonah's stomach.

Jonah groans into the tape and doubles over, held up by Chris's hold on the back of his shirt.

I jump forward, wanting to help my friend, but I'm stopped by the rope tying me to the hoop.

"Come out. Come out. Wherever you are." Chris sings; teasing, taunting.

No movement and Jonah gets another punch to his gut. This time Jonah doesn't straighten up completely, but stays hunched over, moaning and pulling against his restraints.

"Come out!" He delivers a third hit to Jonah's stomach. "Now!" And another.

He waits. Takes a deep breath. Then, he says, "It seems as though your friends don't care about you." And throws him to the side, letting him fall.

I wince as he hits the floor, unable to save himself.

"Maybe they care about you," he says, turning his attention to me.

I wait for him to untie the rope attached to the wall and moves in front of me to pull me up. Before he can tug me to my feet, I jump up and ram my body into his.

Chapter 20

He crashes backwards, and I land on top of him.

That's as much of a plan I came up with. Where do I go from here? I can't attack him with my hands tied behind my back. I can't even stand up.

I'm pushed off him to land on the floor and Nathan helps him to his feet.

Chris yanks me up to my feet and glares at me with a fierce stare. Clenching his jaw. His fingers curl into fists. One fist twisting up the material of my shirt. He takes a step forward, towering over me.

I try to remain mighty and unnerved, staring up at him like he doesn't scare me.

"You're going to regret that," he says in a deep growl.

Before I can brace myself, his fist hits my stomach and I'm forced over in pain. As I begin to straighten up, a second blow forces me back over. My head jerks to the side violently, a burning pain erupting on my cheek.

The hit to my side causes my legs to give out for a second, but Chris holds me up.

"You can only...blame...yourself...for this," he says, dealing several more blows to my head, stomach and side.

Unable to hold myself up for any longer, my knees buckle and give out. Chris looses his hold on me and my body crumbles to the floor.

He drives his foot into my ribs, causing me to roll, coming to a rest on the same side.

I groan and pull against the rope until it cuts into my wrists. Both my knees pull up to my chest to protect my stomach, but they do nothing to save me from the foot that stomps down on my side.

My teeth grit together as I cry out through the tape.

"I guess your friends don't care about you either."

The punch to my cheekbone causes my head to bounce off the floor. A blackness takes over before the world swirls back into my vision, allowing me to see the foot swinging towards me stop. Instead of hitting me, it grounds itself and spins around, pivoting on its toes.

Jonah's groans helps me put two and two together. He had gotten to his feet. Nathan had either let him or not noticed. Jonah made an attempt to attack Chris somehow. That got him punched in the stomach again by Chris.

He throws Jonah to the floor at Nathan's feet. "Do something about him."

With everyone distracted, I use the time to take a quick glance over to Wyatt and Axel's hiding spot. The tiny crack in the cupboard door widens enough for me to see Axel's wide eyes peering out at me.

A nervousness and guilt fills them and I notice his hesitant movement to push past the door.

With one last quick check that Nathan and Chris are still distracted with Jonah, I shake my head at Axel encouraging him to stay hidden.

He sinks back into the hiding spot as Nathan drags Jonah back over to the hoops and ties him to one again.

With Jonah dealt with, Chris turns his attention back to me. He delivers that kick that got interrupted before.

I groan and curl up as much as I can. It's frustrating that I can't protect myself with my hands tied behind my back. All I can do is take the beating and suffer through the pain.

Chris kneels down beside me, grabbing my face to force me to look at him. "This friend cares about you," he says, jabbing his thumb towards Jonah, "but he's not the one who can help you."

He give me a punch to the ribs.

"If the other two want to come out," he says, loud enough to hear throughout the house, sending his fist to my stomach, "they could save you from this."

He stands up and kicks me in the knees. "But they don't seem to care."

I brace myself for the next strike, but it doesn't come. Looking up, I see him staring down at me, holding a knife and wearing a wicked smile. "So, maybe, we should make it a little more interesting."

I glance over at Jonah who watches with wide eyes, and I notice Nathan standing near him, watching, looking uneasy.

Panic flooding my body, I attempt to escape. An attempt that never would have worked. I roll to the side, only to be stopped with a kick to my lower back and a hand gripping my collar.

"You can't get away that easy." He pulls me up to my knees, and rips the tape off my mouth.

I pant from pain and gasp at the air as if I've held my breath for several minutes.

"Go on," he tells me, placing the top of the knife beneath my chin. "Beg them to save you."

I take a deep breath, hold my shoulders high and reply. "No."

His jaw clenches. The knife swipes across my upper arm, cutting through my long sleeved shirt and spilling blood onto it.

My scream bounces off the walls in the room and I fall to the side.

I'm pulled back up my knees. His hand wraps around my arm, squeezing the cut, causing a sharp pain to shoot up my arm. The knife rests on my neck, pushing up into my jaw bone.

He leans down, pulling my head forward with the hand on my back of my neck, pushing the blade further into my skin.

"Wrong answer," he growls, "Try again."

I gulp, gathering courage and preparing for the next strike. "No," I say, loosing some of the confidence I had only moments ago.

He swings stronger, hitting the same arm but a little lower than the first cut.

This time, I manage to stay upright on my knees.

My jaw gets trapped between his fingers, pushing the inside of my mouth against my teeth. The knife points at my eye, shaking from his rage trembling hand.

"Tell them to come out." He lifts his elbow, lowering the knife towards my eye.

"They're not here," I say, my voice failing me at the end.

"Of course they are," he screams. "Now say it."

"We can yell and scream for them to come out all you like," I tell him, trying my hardest to keep my voice steady and strong. "They're. Not. Here." I emphasise my words as much as I can.

"Liar!" He squeeze my jaw, digging his fingers in. "They wouldn't have left you."

"That's exactly what they did," I say.

"Don't lie to me." He releases me from his grasp, swaps the knife over to his other hand, and punches my face without a second of hesitation.

I collapse to the floor.

A kick hits the sore spot on my stomach, a burst of pain exploding through my abdomen.

"I'm not lying," I groan. "You said it yourself, they don't really care about us."

He pulls me back up to my knees. Digging his nails into my shoulder, he leans down to get in my face.

I speak before he can. "They heard you guys coming back," I explain, "and they booked it."

"Their car is still here," he points out. His piercing stare bores through me. "I haven't heard it start. They're still here."

"Yeah," I say, "because people can't use their feet to get away." I have no idea where this confidence has come from but I'm not going to waste it, even if it means I die because of it.

His hand moves to my neck, wrapping around, pulling me closer, his thumb pressing into the soft spot on my throat.

I struggle to breathe.

"Don't use that tone with me," he says, reminding me of my mother. Grinding his teeth and clenching his jaw so his jawbone stands out, he pushes the blade against my cheek. He talks through his teeth. "And if I search this room and find out you are lying to me..." A quick, short flick of the knife, and the blade bites into my skin. I feel a drop of warm blood trailing down my cheek towards my jaw, creating a light tickling sensation. "...I'll cut your tongue out."

Releasing me, I fall backwards. Unable to save myself, I crash down on my lower legs and continue to the floor.

"Keep looking for them!" he yells at his brother.

Nathan scrambles to a side of the room, and begins his search from the beginning.

Like before, Chris stands back, watching and waiting for Nathan to find them as he once again makes he way around the room, moving closer and closer to their hiding spot.

Adrenaline seeps into my veins. I want to jump up and do something to stop them, but what could I do?

He creeps closer, searching.

I have to do something. Anything.

Closer.

I keep my eyes on Chris stood in front of me, watching Nathan search, as I figure out how to get to my feet without using my hands. My heart drums away in my chest. I focus hard to control my breathing and stay silent.

As I stand behind him, I notice a tremble setting-in in my jaw. If he turns around now, he'll get to me first.

I take a step back, brace myself, and rush forward. Using my shoulder first, I ram my body into his back, shoving him hard.

He looses his balance, crashing to the ground, letting out a cry of surprise.

Managing to stay on my feet, I don't hesitate to step over him and run out the room.

"Get him!" I hear Chris scream as I rush into the dark hallway.

With footsteps following behind me, I decide to run upstairs, away from the front door, so the other three can escape if they get the chance.

Chapter 21

I take the stairs three at a time. It's surprisingly hard with my hands bound behind me and the injuries I've sustained, and for a split second, halfway up, I panic that I'm about to face plant but I'm able to keep moving. I make it to the top at the same time I hear my chaser begin to climb the staircase.

The cut on my hip from the car crash throbs, and the ache surrounding my ribs worsens with each harsh breath I take. My head pounds and I wish I could hold my stomach with my arm to stop the radiating pain.

I glance around and quickly decide where to go. A room that already has an open door. Dashing around the double-sized bed, I realised I've blocked myself in with nowhere left to escape to.

I squint through the darkness, looking around for a place to go, but I find nothing. Nowhere I could get to and nowhere they wouldn't find me. Hearing the double set of footsteps approaching the top of the stairs, I face the door, waiting to see if they choose this room first or give me a chance to escape by running into another room.

They glance into my room and upon spotting me standing in the shadows, they step in. Nathan first, and Chris followed behind. While Nathan stands in the doorway, Chris steps past him, walking around the bed, moving towards me.

His head tilts down, making his eyes appear darker and his stare more intense. "You've got a lot of regret coming your way," he snarls at me. Standing in front of me, he reaches out and grabs the back of my neck with a powerful grip.

Pulling me forward, he drags me with him out of the room. Nathan moves aside to let us pass. His nails bite into my neck and dig in further with every movement he forces me to make.

At the top of the staircase, he pulls me to a stop. We stare down them. The moonlight coming through the front door we left open illuminates the bottom half of the stairs.

"This is where it gets fun," he says, digging his fingers in more. I glance out of the side of my eyes to see the nasty smirk he wears, staring at me with a vicious look in his eyes.

Before I can wonder what he means, he releases me and shoves me forward.

My stomach drops. My heart stops. The foot that flies forward to save myself slips over the edge of the stair and my body plummets downwards.

Pain. Pain. And more pain. In my shoulder. On my head. My hip. My shins. Everything hits something.

By the time I reach the bottom half of the stairs, and ache covers my entire body.

A swirl of shadows and light fill my vision until a complete darkness takes over, and when my eyes open again, I'm staring at the wooden floor.

My wrists ache and burn from pulling against the rope. I wonder if they're bleeding yet.

I groan and writhe as Chris walks down the stairs, taking his time, smiling. And Nathan trails behind him.

The cut in my hip now burns with an unbearable intensity, and the two slices on my arm give a fierce sting.

While I lie on my side, curling up and moaning, a foot rests down on my side and pushes me to roll over onto my back, crushing my hands, and keeps pushing me until I'm on my stomach.

The same hand that pushed me down the stairs, picks me up; yanking my arms upwards from behind me. I groan in protest.

I struggle to stay on my feet and Chris's erratic movements don't help, but he makes sure I stay standing, holding me up by the back of my shirt.

My head reels and spins. A pounding comes from deep within, bouncing off every part of my skull. I blink hard, over and over, trying to rid my vision of the black dots that sw m in front of my eyes.

My knees fail to hold me up and continue to buckle no matter home many times Chris pulls me up to stand. This earns me a punch to the gut. After I double over, I'm yanked backwards, causing my head to flop back to look at Chris and his menacing grin.

"Stay with me now," he says, giving me a little shake. "The fun's not over yet."

With his grip removed, I fall and crash to the floor. I'm gripped by my collar and dragged across the floor into the room before I've had a chance to recover.

We reach the doorway and that's where I'm thrown down. He steps into the room without me and screams.

I discover why when I pull my head off the floor and look into the empty room.

I'm unable to stop the sigh of relief from escaping, but I am able to wipe the slight smile from my face before Chris can see it as he whips around to face me.

He storms over. Jaw tense. Fists clenched. Nostrils flaring. His foot makes contact with my cheek bone.

A pain explodes through my head. My body flies to the side until I slam into the door frame, forcing a long groan from me.

"You lied to me!" He steps around me and stomps down as hard as he can on my ankle.

My cries echo around the entire house.

"Where are they?!" He doesn't give me a second to answer before he kicks my leg back, a splitting pain exploding through my shin. "Tell me!" A kick to my lower back sends a shockwave of pain up my spine to my head and down my legs to the end of my toes.

"I—don't—know," I get out between desperate gasps of air.

Another kick sends a crippling pain through me from my side. "That's what you told me before!"

The sound of a car rumbling to a start catches the attention of all three of us, and it stops the attacks.

Chris looks back at the front door, then flicks his head back around to look at Nathan. "Go!" he orders, and Nathan runs over to the front door, stopping in the doorway.

"They're leaving!" he shouts back at us.

"Well, get them!" Chris moves away from me and follows Nathan out the door, taking one last look at me before he disappears into the dark.

I'm not going anywhere, and he knows it. I curl up and shut my eyes. Waves of pain wash over my body.

I don't hear the returning footsteps, I only realise I'm not alone anymore when a hand clamps down over my mouth, stopping the scream that comes along with the jump I give. My eyes spring open.

Jonah holds his finger to his lips.

I relax.

Chapter 22

He leans over me and gets to work, untying the rope around my wrists.

The sound fades out as the car drives away, but before it's gone, a second car revs to life and the wheels spin on the dirt, flicking up rocks.

"Axel's in the car," Jonah explains in a whisper. "We hope both of them will follow. Wyatt is keeping watch outside."

The rope loosens. I'm able to relax a little more without it cutting into my skin.

"Axel will lead them away so we can run," he continues. "And then he'll come back and get us."

The rope falls away from my wrists and I sigh with relief as my shoulders slump forward and I'm able to bring the one arm I'm not lying on around to my front.

Jonah snakes his hand under my arm and helps me sit up. He holds me under both my aching arms and pulls me to my feet. "Let's go."

With my arm over his shoulder and Jonah taking most of my weight to hold me up, we make our way to the front door.

When we make it outside, we see Wyatt climbing up the short staircase, towards the inside of the house. "They both left," he tells us as soon as he spots us.

"Good," Jonah replies, groaning under my weight. His struggles help to remind me of the beating he took and makes me aware of the pain he would be in.

I take as much of my weight off him as I can manage; trying and failing to take all of it from him.

"It's okay," he says, realising what I'm trying to achieve. "Lean on me."

"You sure?" I ask, guilt weighing down on me.

"Yeah," he replies. "Trust me. I'm fine."

I look sideways at him and see him smiling at me.

A smile stretches on my face, noticing his mocking tone. "Ha. Ha. Very funny."

Wyatt reaches us and doesn't hesitate to wrap his arm around me, taking me from Jonah's hold. Jonah let's go and takes the lead.

Wyatt helps me down the stairs and Jonah waits.

"Where are we going?" I ask as we hit the last step.

"Away from here," Jonah answers. "Axel told us to walk towards the forest area, so he can find us, but the other two won't."

Without confirmation, Jonah walks down the dirt road, heading towards the forest. I notice his slight limp and how he holds his stomach with his arm, and can't help but feel bad for leaning on him even though he told me to.

I limp, hopping off my injured ankle as fast as I can, and using Wyatt to hold myself up and keep moving forward.

Every step I take, I feel like I'm crushing Wyatt beneath my weight and I can't help the guilt that swirls inside me.

I continue to take weight off Wyatt, like I did with Jonah, but I don't get very far on my own before I have to crash back down onto Wyatt's shoulder. After several attempts and fails, he says, "Quit trying to be a man, and let me carry you." I give in.

Jonah chuckles and looks back at us. Something over our shoulders catches his attention and he stops. "Here he comes."

Wyatt and I look back to see the beaming headlights in the distance coming our way. I squint as the car comes over a hill and the bright lights shine on us. We stand still, watching it drive past the house and come up the hill towards us, waiting for it to reach us.

"He lost them fast," Jonah says, walking forward to stand next to Wyatt.

As the car speeds up, a second car appears over the hill behind it. The second car flashes its lights from bright to low, bright to low, bright, low. Realisation hits.

"No, he didn't," Wyatt says, echoing my thoughts. "That's not Axel."

In unison, we all turn and run the rest of the way up the hill. Jonah takes off ahead, continuing to limp. Wyatt runs ahead of me. And I take up the rear. Pain shooting through me with each step, I fall behind. Getting further and further away from Wyatt and Jonah.

With nowhere to hide, all I can do is run. And I can't even do that. My ankle throbs, sending a shock-like pain up my leg each time my foot hits the ground. It slows me down, making me the easy target.

Wyatt takes a quick look back at the approaching car and notices how far behind I am. He stops, waiting for me to catch up.

"No," I say, swinging my arm at him. "Keep going."

He ignores me. As I reach him, he steps forward and his arm wraps around me to drag me along the dirt road with him.

I try to shove him off to let him go on ahead. thinking that using me as bait until Axel catches up could be the only way for Jonah and Wyatt to get away. But Wyatt holds onto me, refusing to leave me behind.

Struggling to stay upright. Stumbling often. Unable to run fast. I slow Wyatt down, but the only reason I'm still on my feet is because of Wyatt's arm around me, holding me up. Still, I wish he would let me go, and take the advantage to get away.

Jonah looks back at us and follows Wyatt's actions. Stopping. Waiting. Staying back to help.

With him on my other side, we're able to move a little faster, but still not as fast as they both could run without me.

We hear the car coming, crunching over the dirt road. The head-lights growing brighter until we reach the top of the hill and begin our descent, leaving us only with moonlight to guide us.

"This way," Wyatt says, leading us off the road and through the tall dead grass, stumbling over rocks the size of bowling balls.

Scanning the darkness for a sign of where we're heading, I spot nothing until we get closer. A drop in the earth, creating a short cliff edge.

I know we have to make it there before their car comes over the hill and sees us, so I push myself further, battling through the pain, allowing Wyatt and Jonah to run faster.

Chapter 23

As we reach the drop in the earth, Jonah and Wyatt let me go. Wyatt jumps down first. Jonah groans as he squats down, and he takes Wyatt's outstretched hand to help him jump.

Taking a deep breath, preparing to endure whatever pain comes, I squat down to sit on the edge, and with Wyatt and Jonah's help by grabbing my arms, I lift up and they help lower me down over the edge. A sharp ache zips up and down my arms until I'm standing on my better leg.

With the cliff edge only reaching up to my waist, we have to crouch down to hide ourselves.

We wait; listening to the car drive up the road towards us, and our harsh and rapid breaths after our desperate run.

As the car nears our hiding spot, we wait to hear them to drive past, but instead the car stops. Hearing the car doors open, I hold my breath.

"You think you're smarter than me?!" Chris calls out.

My heart halts and plummets.

Their footsteps move closer, yet slow.

"What do we do now?" Jonah asks in a whisper that I can almost not hear.

"Run?" Wyatt suggests in the same quiet voice.

"We're not going to get far with Dorian," says Jonah.

He's right. We all can't escape, but they could. Now's the time to act as bait. "You two run," I tell them. "I'll make them come after me instead."

"What's with you and self-sacrifice recently?" asks Jonah.

"You got any better ideas?" I say.

Before either one of them can offer any, Chris jumps down from the short cliff edge and lands in front of us, already facing us. My body jerks in surprise and I push myself backwards, the rocky cliff face digging into my back.

"You know," he says, the darkness hiding the expression on his face. "I really love how stupid you all are." He takes one step towards us, forcing us to crane our necks to keep our eyes on him. "It makes it that much easier to catch you."

He reaches down, grabs the front of Jonah's shirt, and pulls him up. "Time to go," he says. Lifting him up by his shirt, he throws him backwards, up onto the top of the short drop.

I hear Jonah roll on the ground, collecting dust and dirt on his clothes.

"Take him," Chris orders to his brother.

Footsteps rush forward, and I listen to him drag Jonah to his feet, taking him back to the still running car.

Next, he chooses Wyatt. Treating him the same way. Yanking him up before pushing him against the cliff. He waits for Nathan to deal with Jonah, refusing to let him go without the escort.

A grunt sounds from above and behind me, and I panic, unable to tell if it was Jonah or Nathan.

I get an answer when I hear footsteps running and Chris jumps forward and shouts, "Get him!" Under his breath, while Nathan chase after Jonah, he mumbles, "Useless piece of shit."

I'm pulled up. With the sudden movement, a bolt of pain shoots through me, causing me to wince.

He holds onto both of us, but allows me to look back to see Jonah leading Nathan over the hill and disappearing into the approaching light of Axel's car.

As soon as they're both out of sight, the grip on my shirt loosens and when I turn around, I'm faced with a knife pointed at me.

"Get up there," he says to me, using the knife to point to the ledge. "And don't pull anything, or..." He drags Wyatt in front of him and places the knife to his throat. "...he'll be dead before he hits the ground."

Without hesitation, I lean back against the cliff and hoist myself up, screwing my face up and grinding my teeth. Getting to my feet, he pushes the knife into Wyatt's neck, waiting to see what I do next. When I don't do anything, he nudges Wyatt forward. "Jump up." He looks at me. "Don't move."

Wyatt follows orders, pushing himself up on his hands and jumping up onto the ledge.

Before Wyatt can straighten up, Chris leaps up beside him and returns the knife to Wyatt's throat.

Standing behind him, he looks at me and says, "Walk."

I limp over to the black car, heading towards its side until he says, "Back of the car." Using this time, I glance down the road to see Nathan still chasing after Jonah, but Axel in the car has almost reached them and I'm certain Axel will get to him first.

Stopping at the back of the car, I turn to watch Chris walk with a stiff-walking, nervous Wyatt.

He stands to my side, facing the back of the car, and orders me to, "Open it."

I pull the door up.

When he orders me to get in, I hesitate. He pushes the knife into Wyatt's neck more, forcing his head to lift. The blade begins to slide to the side.

"Okay. Okay," I say, and climb into the back of the car. This isn't a good idea. But what else can I do?

He lets the knife fall away and shoves Wyatt into the car. He climbs in beside me and the door slams shut, closing us in in pitch black darkness.

Over the sound of the car's rumble, Wyatt whispers to me, "I don't have a plan for this."

"That's okay," I say. "Neither do I."

Moments pass.

Without thinking about it when I got in, I chose to lie on my side with the cut on my hip. Now, it aches and burns w th intensity, and I'm not sure how much longer I can bare it, but in the small space, I don't think I can move.

From the outside, I can just make out the words Chris shouts. "You are the most useless person on the face of the earth."

I don't hear the reply, only a muffled voice, drowned out by the sound of the engine.

"Hurry up," Chris says. "Get in the car."

Seconds later, we hear a door open and close followed by a second door. Then, the car drives off.

Chapter 24

W e drive. Each bump and bounce sends a searing pain through my entire body. It explodes through my bones and burns to the end of every nerve.

I'm sure when the car stops, they'll kill us, and there's nothing we will be able to do about it, but I'm wishing this to be there now. I want the bouncing to stop. The pain rises to an unbearable point and doesn't stop there.

I try to keep from groaning and crying out but the longer it goes on the more I can't help it.

When the car slows and pulls to a stop, I relax my tense body and breathe a breath of relief.

With a last minute idea, I ask Wyatt, "Is there anything we could use as a weapon?"

I hear Wyatt's hand scuffle around on the floor, searching for something, and I do the same on my side.

"Nope," he says. "I got nothing."

"Same," I tell him.

"So, we're dead."

"Yep." I crack a smile and hear a single huff of a laugh come from Wyatt.

The engine cuts off and the car doors open and shut.

I gather myself, preparing for whatever comes next. Taking a few deep breaths. Calming my mind. Accepting the lack of chances for escape. Whatever happens next, I'll have to deal with it.

The door flies open. I don't remember the moonlight being that bright before. It shines around the dark silhouette of Chris, staring down at us, the knife in hand.

"Get out," he says, pointing the knife at us, stepping back to give us room.

Wyatt lifts himself up and drags himself out of the car. Chris grabs his wrist before he's gotten out, and as soon as both his feet hit the ground, he spins him around and holds the knife to his throat.

I climb out, holding in the cry of pain I want to let out as I lift my leg up and out.

Chris clearing his throat catches my attention but I realise it's not for me when Nathan moves forward and grabs a hold of my arm.

"Don't think I won't spill your blood right now," Chris tells us. "If either of you run, fight, or doing anything stupid, I won't hesitate." He pulls the knife in closer, pressing the blade deep into his skin without drawing blood.

We're forced to walk, with both of our captures behind us. Wyatt and Chris in front, me and Nathan following behind them.

I notice Chris dragging and throwing Wyatt around more than Nathan does to me. He allows me to lead most of the time.

Choosing our path around the trees. His grip stays firm but loose, unlike Chris's vice-like grip.

I only have two problems. One being I'm forced to walk faster than I can manage. Nathan refuses to let my limp and my pain slow us down. He pushes me forward, making me keep up with Chris's long strides.

The second: we're walking to our graves.

Nathan stops when Chris throws Wyatt down onto the forest floor. He turns to me, glaring, and storms over. Pulling me from Nathan's grasp, he says, "Grab the other one."

Nathan walks over to Wyatt and helps him up by his arm, barely holding onto him.

The knife rests on the edge of my jaw, the point of it jabbing into my cheekbone. His fingernails stab into my neck bones.

"You should have stayed away," he says, dragging the cold blade down to push against the pulse in my throat.

It begins to slide. Stinging. Biting. I panic. My heart races. This it it. I feel a drop of blood fall down my neck. Warm.

My last breath gets stuck in my throat.

Chris's dark eyes pierce through me. His wicked smirk sends chills through every bone in my body.

Time slows. The cold wind stops. Crickets quiet their chirps until silence surrounds us. Every swaying tree freezes, and every twirling leaf hangs still, forcing the moonlight to quit the dancing patterns it created on the forest floor.

The only thing that keeps its movement is that drop of blood rolling down my neck. As it hits my collarbone, the blade continues to slide. Cutting my skin apart.

Chris's eyes shut tight. His head flops to the side. It continues to fall, his body following. The knife leaves my neck. I watch, unmoving, as he falls to the floor. His body hits the earth, his head bouncing off the ground, and that's when all movement regains it's normal speed.

The trees sway. Moonlight twinkles through the fluttering leaves. Wind blows around me. The cricket's chirps return, growing louder. Hot breath rushes out past my lips and cold air fills my lungs. My heart drums strong and fast, echoing to my ears.

The rock drops from Nathan's hand, landing with a single thump on the dirt.

Chris groans. His hand moves up to his head, pressing down on a small patch of red. "What the hell," he moans, looking up at his wide eyed brother. "Why the hell would you do that?!"

"This isn't right," he replies.

Chris drags himself up to his feet, turning to face Nathan. "Are you kidding me?!" His hands curl into fists. The knife rests amongst the leaves on the ground.

"I never wanted to hurt anyone," he says, standing his ground but looking like he wants to run. "I just wanted to give my daughter a better life."

"You created this situation." Chris steps forward, forcing Nathan to cower back. "I'm just trying to get us out of it."

Nathan tries his best to stand strong and unflinching but his rapid blinking and the constant swallowing he does gives away his nerves and fear. "You created this situation by coming here and making it worse."

"Don't you dare blame all this on me!" Thump. Chris thrusts his hand into Nathan's chest, shoving him back. "You started it all by kidnapping a useless child for a pathetic reason."

I step back away from them, moving slow to not make any sound that would give me away, never taking my eyes off the two of them. The more distance I create the better. I don't want to be anywhere near him after this.

Nathan recovers after his stumble only to be pushed back again. "So, back off..."He receives another hit. "... and let me handle it."

As I take my forth slow step away, Chris whips back around to face me. He picks up the knife and marches towards me. His hand wraps around my arm, gripping as tight as he can manage and swings the knife over his opposite shoulder.

Before he can swoop it across my neck, the rock makes a second connection to his head.

He hits the floor. This time the knife stays in his grasp.

I'm gripped around my arm and pulled to the side. "Come on." Nathan drags me over to Wyatt.

He stands frozen with shock as I would. "Go. Go. Go," he says, pushing Wyatt and I away from Chris who moans in pain on the floor.

My feet refuse to work on their own for several steps, and I notice Wyatt reacting the same way. We stumble and move from Nathan's constant shoves until our brains start to work again and were able to turn and run. Running as fast as we can.

Wyatt runs ahead, but refuses to run too far and leave me behind.

I try to take longer steps to compensate for the limp that holds me back, but it doesn't work. Especially with Nathan still behind me, pushing me forward, not caring about the pain I'm in.

Where are we going? What's his plan? Is he letting us go?

"Where would your friends have gone?" he asks between harsh breaths.

I don't answer. Neither does Wyatt. Why does he care? What does he want with them?

"Will they come back for you," he continues, "or will I have to take you somewhere."

Is he—Is he really—actually helping us?

"Uh..." Wyatt says, sounding unsure, using the excuse of panting to avoid the question.

"I didn't want anyone to get hurt," says Nathan. "And I'm sick of—I—I I certainly don't want anyone to die. You need to get out of here before he gets to you." He gives me another shove as I begin to slow, causing me to stumble, but I'm able to stay on my feet. "Where can I take you?"

"Our friends won't have left," Wyatt tells him. "They'll come back to get us."

"Okay. Good."

I'm not sure if telling him that was a good idea. What if he has a secret plan? He could just want to know their whereabouts to kill them.

Although, he did actually hit his brother over the head with a rock. Twice. That was not faked. I heard the thump it made on contact. Would he do that just to kill us himself?

I wonder what happened to Chris? I never got a chance to see if he died or got up. Did the hit knock him unconscious? Or is he chasing us right now? I hope he's bleeding to death.

"I'm sorry for all of this." He doesn't speak loud enough for Wyatt to hear him from further ahead, so I know he's only talking to me.

"I didn't want any of this," he continues, "I just wanted to help my daughter."

I want to turn and punch him as hard as I can in the face. You have no idea if she's yours. Instead, I say, "There's better ways to do that."

"I know," he breathes. "She told me all about how you and her mother never gave her the time of day. I thought neither of you would miss her if I took her."

What kind of sociopath thinks that they can just take a child and no one will care? "You were wrong," I tell him. I know Misty never got much attention from Mum and I, and I always pushed her to the side, but that doesn't mean I'm okay with her being taken by a strange maniac.

"Clearly," he says.

I can't forgive him. I won't. A simple apology doesn't make this better. What would make this better would be him handing Misty back over to me and then he drops dead.

Chapter 25

The conversation ends, and moments later I spot their car in the distance, standing out from the shadows only by the white headlights that reflect the moon's light.

I'm able to see the outline of the car as a light appears behind it. Two bright headlights shine over the hill and stop behind it.

I only spot Axel and Jonah's figures as they run towards us, stepping in the way of the headlights.

Spotting us, they both slow, stop, then run again. Unsure as to whether they should stop or not.

"Get in the car!" Wyatt screams at them, and with that they turn and run back to the car.

Axel and Jonah stop as they pull open the car doors, looking back at Wyatt, Nathan, and I.

"What's going on?" Axel screams over the car door.

"Get in the car!" I shout back.

They don't listen. They stare at me; watching me limping, struggling to run, screwing up my face from the pain that stabs into my ankle.

"What about him?!" Jonah shouts, gesturing to Nathan.

"Don't worry about me," Nathan cries out. "Just get out of here."

Adrenaline pumps through my veins, kick-starting my heart, and making my head spin the closer I get to the car.

I can't run fast enough. The car seems so far away. I want to get in, slam the door shut and drive away as soon as I can. Then, I remember the reason I'm out here in the first place.

I pull to a stop. My ankle screams at me as though it's about to snap. Whipping around, Nathan has to dig his heels into the ground to stop from crashing into me. "What about my sister?" I ask. "Where is she?"

He blinks at me, processing my words, before he stutters out his answer. "I—uh—I don't know."

"What do you mean, you don't know?" I say, taking a step closer to be as intimidating as possible. It doesn't work too well with my scrunched up face and the groan at the end of my words.

"She ran off and hid," he tells me. "I don't know where she is."

Liar!

"Mate," Axel says, catching my attention, "Get in the car."

"No," I say, looking back at Nathan. "I'm not leaving her here."

He holds his hands up. "I don't know where-" he begins.

Axel cuts him off, raising his voice and speaking as if he's talking to a young child that won't do as they're told. "Get in the car, Dorian."

"No," I reply, without bothering to look back. "Dead or alive. I'm taking her."

Before Nathan can reply, Axel shouts, "Dorian!"

Hesitant to break eye contact with Nathan, I turn to face him when Nathan refuses to say anything.

He gives me a sharp stare and says, "Get. In. The. Car."

I can hear the desperation in his voice, something telling me there's more to what he's saying. Trusting my friend, I back away. I hope whatever plan he has, it works.

I turn and walk towards the car. Axel and Jonah watch me from behind the open car doors, and Wyatt waits a moment to make I'm not going to change my mind before he also turns and walks the rest of the way.

As Wyatt reaches the front of the car, Jonah jumps to the side, out from in front of the door, and gestures to Nathan still standing where I left him behind me. "Hurry!"

I whip around, searching for whatever Jonah has seen. It takes me a moment to spot the movement in darkness behind Nathan.

Nathan turns and looks behind as I realise what I'm looking at.

Chris charges towards us. His stare locked onto me.

Nathan throws himself in front of him as he nears him. Chris darts back and forth, trying to get around, but Nathan matches every movement.

Frustrated, Chris shoves his brother to the side. "Get out of the way," he growls.

Before he can storm past, Nathan jump back in front, blocking him from us again. "No," he says, and Chris's face turns red.

He tries to push past, but Nathan manages to keep him back, infuriating him so much it looks as though he could explode at any second.

"You need to pick a side," Chris says, giving up on his attempts to get around, and stands in his face instead.

"No," he replies, moving back to gain his personal space back. "I don't."

"Traitor," he spits at him.

"I'm not against you." Nathan raises his hands. "I'm just against you killing."

"You forced me into this!" Chris replies, shoving him back once.

Nathan stumbles and saves himself. "There are better ways to deal with this."

"You wanna lecture me on how to deal with things properly?!" Another shove. And another step towards us. "Get out of my way or I'll beat you to a bloody pulp."

"No," Nathan says. "We can fix this a different way."

Chris looks down, takes a deep breath in through his nose, and raises his head with a scowl on his face. "You've been a thorn in my side for years now. I won't feel bad about this."

He pushes forward, knocking Nathan backwards. Nathan manages to stay on his feet and pushes back against Chris.

They wrestle with each other, and deliver multiple hits.

Chris shoves Nathan, and Nathan swings his fist into his head. Recovering fast, Chris slams his hands into Nathan's stomach, forcing him back again. I see Chris's head fly back but I don't see the hit. A crack can be heard from the punch to Nathan's jaw. Ouch.

Axel catches my attention. "Dorian!" I look back to see him gesturing me to the car.

Remembering where I am, I turn and walk towards the car. I should have used their distraction to get out of here sooner, but focusing on the two boys scrabbling made me forget about any threat.

The other three stand beside the car, watching the fight as I hobble towards them. Jonah and Axel still stay behind the open doors. Wyatt stands beside Jonah.

Nearing them, I hear a grunt sound louder than the rest and then silence. Curiosity wins over the need to get in the car, and I stop and look behind me.

Both of them stand still, and as close as they can get to each other. I can't see Nathan's face. Chris wears a strong, intense expression. Unfaltering.

Neither of them move. Not a single blink. Frozen. Staring into each other's eyes.

I should move. Get in the car. Leave. But I'm stuck, as if time has stopped, leaving us all frozen. Watching.

Chris reaches his hand up to Nathan's shoulder, and gives him a light shove, forcing him to gasp and stumble back. My gasp gets stuck in my throat as my lungs close off, refusing any oxygen I try give them.

Chris holds the knife tight in his hand. The blade dripping red. It doesn't tremble or shake. He keeps it's steady and holds it firm, as if he's used it for nothing other than chopping tomatoes.

As Nathan continues to stagger away from his brother, he turns, and places his hand on his stomach, pulling it away to leave a dark stain and red on his fingers. I notice his face pale and his knees begin to shake.

There's nothing we could do to help him. He's already halfway gone.

His knees buckle, and his legs give out, collapsing under him. He crumbles to the floor, landing on his back.

I watch him struggle to breathe, and his hands clutch at his stomach, unsure as to what he should do. His rapid breaths slow until he takes one more and releases it slow. Then, he's still. Too still. Dead.

My head whirls. The thump of my heart pounds in my head. Wh—What just—What just happened? I can't believe anything my eyes just witnessed. He...killed his brother. Killed. His own brother!

His head flicks up to look at me. The expression on his face unchanged. He doesn't show guilt. Or remorse. Or the slightest bit of sadness. It's his brother, and he does care.

Keeping the sharp look, he starts towards me.

If he killed his brother without a problem, what will he do to me.

Chapter 26

He runs.

A powerful wave of panic slams down over top of me like a boulder but that doesn't stop me from turning and running. I run as fast as my injuries will allow.

The car is right there; it's so close, but he's closer, and with my pain, he's faster. I can hear him gaining on me. Catching me up.

I see the three of my friends in front me, standing beside the open doors, encouraging me to run faster, waiting to jump in and go when I get there.

I'm almost there. Just a little further. Run. Run. Please don't fall. Run. Faster! Pain like electric shocks surges through my body. Don't fall. I'm almost there. Run faster!

The slight touch on my shoulder sends white-hot jolts of fear through me. His grip pushes me down, and in the half a second I have before the world becomes a blur, I see my three friends jump from the car and run towards us.

I hit the ground. He lands on top of me. The two of us roll around in the dirt together. He loses his grip on me and he rolls on ahead. We both come to a stop.

With nowhere else to go but back, I get to my feet and run further away from the car and my only chance at safety.

I take two steps. Chris launches himself at me to grab my ankle. My knees hit the ground and I faceplant. Dirt in my mouth.

I kick and thrash around, attempting an escape, but failing as Chris pulls me towards him. A bite of pain shocks me and without looking, I know he's sliced at my ankle with the knife.

I let out a scream and kick at his hands. As I look down at him, I manage to make contact and kick the knife out of his hold.

I lose it in the darkness as it flies up into the air. A second later, I hear it plop onto the earth to the side of us. Too far out of reach.

At least he can't reach it either.

Wyatt runs up behind him. Chris swings around, elbowing him in his stomach.

As Wyatt stumbles back, clutching his stomach, Chris's grip loosens and I'm able to take the short-lived advantage to pull my leg from him.

He chases after my leg while I get to my feet and when I get away from him, he jumps up too.

The four of us stand around Chris. Each of us waiting for someone else to make the first move. When nobody does, I swallow hard and go for it.

While he glances at Wyatt, with his back towards me. I leap forward. I notice Wyatt takes his eyes off Chris for half a second to look at me instead.

No. No. Please don't notice him. Stay turned—

Chris whirls around and his fist flies into my face before I can begin to swing at him.

Blackness. White sparks. Moonlight. I stay standing. How? Pain fizzles in my cheekbone. My fingers reach for the spot. I check them for blood but they come away clean.

Looking back, I see Chris shove Axel away, and Jonah already on the ground.

Wyatt runs at Chris who jumps to the side and shoves Wyatt past him, letting him fall.

Axel jumps forward. Chris prepares. Axel will go down. Then, it's my turn. I can—I'll wait for the—

Chris grabs Axel by the front of his shirt and swings him around so he comes barrelling towards me. We crash into each other and fall to the ground.

He punches Jonah's jaw and spins around to kick Wyatt in his side.

How is he—We haven't landed a shot. How—What kind of ninja warrior is he?

Axel gets to his feet, runs at him, and throws a punch. Chris dodges the swing and returns the favour right away.

I'm up as Axel goes down. Not for long. I receive a hit to my gut, forcing me to double over, and a punch to my jaw. Crack. It knocks me down.

How could we possibly win this?

I look up in time to see Wyatt being pulled by his arm to land on top of me.

Jonah's arm gets stopped mid-swing and yanked, forcing him to stand beside Chris. Without a second to wonder, Chris raises his own arm up and slams his elbow down in the middle of Jonah's forearm.

I wince and look away.

His blood-curdling scream pierces through the atmosphere and echoes far into the distance.

Chris lets go and shoves him back, so he stumbles away, clutching his arm.

Oh, shit! We're screwed. He's brutal and apparently unbeatable.

Axel comes up behind Chris and gets an arm swung into his head before he can make a move.

On our feet, Wyatt and I rush up behind him and grab him as he whips around to face us.

I follow Wyatt's lead; gripping the front of his shirt, pushing him back, and running forwards.

Fall. Fall. Fall!

But he doesn't. He stays standing, running backwards. After several steps, he digs his heels in and pushes back. Moving to the side, he lets me fall forward.

I tumble to the ground. He gives Wyatt two punches to his stomach, one to his side, and one across his jaw. Letting him go, Wyatt drops to the ground.

I had seconds to stand up. To prepare. I didn't use them. Instead, I sat on the ground, watching, waiting patiently for my turn to be beaten. I'm an idiot.

He shifts his attention to me and there's not much I can do now to defend myself. I push myself up to stand, but I'm too late.

Shit! What do I do? What do I do?

With a kick towards my head, I drop back down and block it with my upper arm. Another strike aims for the side of my ribs. My elbow takes the blow, sending a jarring shock up my arm that takes my breath away and knocks me to the side.

Seeing another kick coming, I curl up to protect myself. When 't never hits, I take a peak up at him and find him gone.

He stumbles backwards with Axel clinging to his back.

Yes! Finally! Let's do this. We can do this!

I get to my feet and run. He spins in circles, reaching behind his head, trying to grab Axel. Axel hangs from his neck, dangling down to avoid the grasping hands.

I run up with his back turned. When he spins to face me, I punch. Into his stomach. Putting all the power I hold into it. My knuckle crack against his solid abdomen.

He groans through his teeth, giving me enough satisfaction to force a slight smile onto my face.

Ha ha. Yeah!

He steps back and crashes into a tree, crushing Axel against it.

Axel groans but holds on. He pulls himself up and wraps his arms around his neck, squeezing tight.

Chris gasps and scratches at Axel's arms, creating faint red lines.

Recognising a second opportunity, I go in for another punch. Chris grabs my wrist, stopping me as my knuckles brush against his grey shirt.

Oh no.

His fingers squeeze around my wrist, cutting the circulation and crushing my bones. Breathless and red-faced, his jaw clenched. His eyes sharpen. Darken.

I'm out of breath. Tired and sore. Sweat stings my eyes.

He pulls me in and wraps his hands around my neck. His thumbs pushed into the soft spot, closes off my throat. Air can't get in or out. Smashing my hands down on his arms only makes him tighten his grip.

He steps forward, pulling me in. I tug on his arms. Pain grows beneath his thumbs, feeling like a rock stuck in my throat. I fight for air. Gasping. The strain travels down to my lungs. Burning. Like fire.

He slams back. Axel grunts.

Darkness creeps into the edges of my vision. My mouth wide open. Tears in my eyes. Clutching his arms, my strength weakens.

Chris looks to the side. He tosses me back. Airways open, I suck in. The air filling my lungs gets stuck halfway in.

On the ground, on my hands and knees, I cough and splutter. My hand rubs at the tender spot on my throat.

Looking back, Wyatt falls to the ground. Chris slams back. Axel groans, looses his grip, and crashes down to the base of the tree.

No! He's up. We're all down. He has the advantage now. Or were—Did we ever have—

Wyatt, gripped by the front of his shirt, takes a punch to the face. Blood falls from his nose. A second punch smears it.

With one more cough, I crawl forward, sit back, and kick him behind one of his knees. His leg gives out, forcing him to his knees, and he pulls Wyatt down with him.

Axel jumps to his feet. I drag myself up. Chris reacts faster. He gets up and delivers a kick to Axel's stomach, sending him down.

Wyatt stays down. Holding his face. Bloody. Groaning. In the dirt.

How are we going—

My head hits the ground. Blackness. Everything swirls back. Patterns and shapes, colours and shadows. Chris's eyes bore into me from above. The smile on his face flips my stomach. His body on top of mine crushes me. I'm out of breath. I suck in. No, I can't. I can't. His hands squeeze my neck.

I'm not sure how long my hands have been scratching and hitting at his arms, but with each second that passes, they grow weaker and slower. My vision blurs.

This is dying—death. I'm dying. I can't do—I'm not stronger—I can't. Misty—Did he do this to—I can't—he—I'm—he—

Pain settles on top of my chest, aching and gnawing at me from inside. It spreads over my entire chest, trailing down my sides and draping around to my back like a massive snake wrapped around me. Crushing. Squeezing. My lungs shrivel up, giving me the sensation of my chest caving in.

A foot soars into the little vision I have left and I get to see it connect with Chris's face.

My airways open and my lungs don't waste any time filling up with as much as as they can take. The darkness fades away. The pain vanishes. My chest opens up, and gets flooded with relief, feeling lighter.

Chapter 27

I fall into a coughing fit. Breathe. Let me breathe. In. Out. I wheeze. My throat throbs. Breathing hurts.

Chris lays on the ground beside me. Groaning and moaning. He touches his hand to his head, and groans louder.

He flick his glare up to see who kicked him. Jonah, still holding onto his arm, swallows hard. He steps back as Chris leaps to his feet.

My stomach swirls with uncontrollable nerves watching them both. Chris steps forward, and Jonah steps back. He mimics every move Chris makes, clutching his arm against himself. Jonah doesn't stand a chance. He's screwed. Chris will—

Or maybe not. Wyatt steps between the two of them, already swinging for Chris's head.

Chris leans back, dodging the hit by a whisker. The second strike lands in the palm of his hand. With the same hand, he grips it and yanks him towards him. In the same movement, Chris sends other his fist into Wyatt's stomach.

Doubled over, he's pushed away, towards me, and collapses.

I move to get up, but stop when a glint of light beside me catches my attention. I stare at the knife. Moonlight bouncing off it. Blood staining half of the blade to the tip.

Do I—Should I—I don't want—but—He could—If I don't grab it, Chris—finds it—he could get it. Then what? What would we—How could we beat him? Without it.

I reach down and pause. My hand hovering over it. I look over at the scrabbling group.

Chris keeps moving towards Jonah and doesn't stop when Axel takes Wyatt's spot in the middle.

Axel, in front of Jonah, dodges a punch, jumping back. The second one flies in too fast for him to avoid. It strikes his chest with a hard thump. Another hit to his jaw makes a cracking sound. And down Axel goes.

Oh God. My turn.

I lower my hand, finding the knife without looking. Picking it off the earth, I hold it in a loose grip. My hand shakes. I don't want to do this.

I get up, moving quietly.

Chris grabs Jonah's injured arm. His scream drowns out the sound of a stick snapping under my shoe. He takes a punch to the face, and Chris lets him fall.

I'm not close enough to act when he turns to me. I freeze.

Oh shit. What do I—what do I do now?

Flicking his eyes down to the knife in my hand, he moves towards me.

Wyatt stands up, between me and him, and Chris takes his eyes from me for a second to look at him but doesn't stop.

Wyatt prepares himself, waiting for him to get close enough, but Chris acts faster. Rushing in and swinging at him first. Wyatt copies Chris's move; grabbing his hand before he gets hit.

Yes!

Chris uses Wyatt's same arm and pulls him in. In a swift movement, he raises his elbow up into Wyatt's face. He continues forward, eyes back on me, as Wyatt drops.

I gulp. My hand trembles and shakes as I lift it up to point the blade at him.

"You gonna stab me, are ya?" he asks, still moving.

I want to say yes. I want to appear threatening. But I know I won't stab him. I don't have the guts. So, I say nothing.   keep it pointed at him and when he gets closer I do the next best thing, I swing it up at him.

His forearm hits mine and the knife falls from my loose hold. Before I can see where it falls, I get a punch to my face.

When I straighten up, he has the knife in his hand. Swinging his arm out wide to hit me.

I suck in a breath. Probably my last.

Everything plays out in slow motion. Seconds pass, but I could swear I live through years in this single moment.

His thumb rests on the blunt side of the blade. The edge stained red. It gets closer. Coming for my head. My neck. Slow, yet too fast to blink.

His aim falls off course as Axel comes up and shoves him to the side. Falling, his arm follows through, missing my head. The tree to his side catches him. He grunts on impact.

We all wait for his next action, but he stays facing the tree. He doesn't move. Staring at the tree trunk. Almost hugging it.

He pulls away. Moving slow. Making a gradual turn.

I gasp. The blade handle sticks to the outside of his chest. A dark stain surrounds it. From what I can tell, he's not breathing. He gives each of us one last glance, lingering on me at the end before his stare drifts off into the distance.

His knees buckle and give out. He stays kneeling for a moment before falling forward to the ground.

I flinch and look away before I see the handle hit the ground before he does.

When I look back at him, he's face down and unmoving. Dead.

Hearing Axel, beside me, start breathing again, I'm reminded to do the same.

Chapter 28

No one moves. No one speaks. Silence consumes us all. Our wide-eyed stares stay glued on the fallen figure in front of us.

I can't find a single word to say. Every thought escapes my mind.

None of this feels real. It has to be a dream. No. A nightmare. Nothing else could explain how I got here. How any of this could happen. This can't be real life. I'm not here. I'm not part of this. I didn't just watch two people get murdered right in front of me. That doesn't happen in real life. Not in my life.

Those people aren't dead. Neither of them are real. They don't exist. My mind made them up to play the villains in this dream. I'm asleep in my bed, having a vivid nightmare before my alarm clock wakes me and takes me away from this place. Soon. Anytime now. I won't have to live through this much longer.

Wake up. Wake up. Please. Wake up!

The body doesn't disappear. None of the scenery changes. No blaring sounds fill the atmosphere. I don't wake up.

I glance around at the others, all of them stare at the body. Blood pours from Wyatt's nose. Jonah holds his arm. Axel rubs his fingers on his jaw that already shows evidence of a bruise beneath the red smears.

Reaching up, my fingers feel at the spot where his thumbs had pressed in on my airways. An ache still lingers. My split lip stings and the side of my ribs holds onto a nagging pain.

I don't need to pinch myself. I have enough pain to tell me that I need to accept this moment as reality.

Axel breaks the stillness, confirming for me that the world hadn't frozen. He walks towards Chris. Wincing. Limping. Kneeling down, he places two fingers on his neck and waits. He shifts them around. Here. There Searching. After several seconds—or minutes, or days—he pulls his hand away and looks back at us. "He's dead," he confirms.

I hear Jonah release a breath. "Now what?"

"We call the police," Wyatt says, wiping blood from his face.

Axel stands up. "And tell them I just murdered someone?"

"It was self-defence," Jonah says.

"Doesn't matter." Axel gestures down to Chris. "I still killed him."

"Technically," I say. "He killed himself."

"I shoved him." Axels voice grows a little louder.

"But he," Wyatt points down at the fallen figure at Axel's feet, "was holding the knife."

Axel shakes his head and frowns. "But the cops won't believe he just stabbed himself willingly."

"So," says Wyatt. "We're supposed to just leave both of them out here?"

"Sounds good to me," I say under my breath, earning a small chuckle from Jonah.

After everything they've done, I couldn't care if the birds and wildlife picked them to pieces until there's nothing left. They deserve it.

"We can't do that," Wyatt says, crushing my dreams. "Someone will find them eventually, and they'll figure out we were here."

"How would they?" Axel asks. He takes a step forward, rubbing his red wrist.

"Our fingerprints will be all over the house," Wyatt explains.

"We could scrub it clean."

"Seriously?" Jonah says with disgust. "I don't even clean my own bedroom."

"Axel, we aren't in the wrong," says Wyatt. "This isn t your fault. The cops will see that as much as we do."

"No, they won't," Axel replies, throwing his arms up. "They'll look for someone to blame, and there's no one else but us."

"There's the two dead guys they could blame," Jonah says.

I can't stop the slight smile from pushing its way onto my face.

Axel rolls his eyes. Looking down at Chris, he asks, "Can we move away from him?"

I glance down at the lifeless body. Shivers rush up my spine. Yes. Yes please.

Everyone gives a nod, and without a word, we move away from the body, walking towards the car still shining light on us from a distance.

I have no idea what we should do. Wyatt makes a good point. If we don't tell someone about this, we'll look guiltier when they figure out we were here. But on the other hand, I don't care about them. They can rot. They would do the same for us.

Axel breaks the silence. "I say we just get in the car and drive away."

I wish it could be that easy. That we could just drive away and never have to worry about this night again. Everything solves itself. None of us have to think about it ever again or deal with any consequences. But that won't happen. If we leave, the problems of this night will follow. We can't escape.

"Axel, you didn't do anything wrong," Wyatt reassures. "The evidence will prove that. Your fingerprints won't be on the knife."

"Mine are." I touched the knife. I held it. I can be blamed for stabbing him, and my fingerprints will prove it.

An ill feeling settles in my stomach, weighing it down like lead. I could go to jail for killing someone that killed themselves. Could I be blamed for Nathan's death too? Would the police believe a murder-suicide with the four of us still standing around here? Even if they believed our story, would Axel still get the blame because he pushed him? Or would I get the blame for coming out here in the first place?

I should have called the police and let them deal with both of them at the beginning. Maybe then no one would have died. Maybe Misty would have been saved and returned. Or maybe they would have been spooked and killed her before the police could get them.

Did I make the right choice? Is this my fault? Did I make the situation worse? Was it a mistake to drag my friends into this situation? If I never had called them and told them to come get me, they would still be at Jonah's, wondering when I was going to arrive. They would be safe and innocent. I should have kept them out of this.

"We could go back and wipe the handle," suggests Jonah.

My fear has me considering it.

"That will make us suspicious for sure." No one replies to Wyatt.

We stay quiet as we approach Nathan still lying lifeless on the ground. I stare at his body as we pass until I have to force my eyes away when my stomach flips and twists into tight knots.

The headlights blind me, and I have to squint to see where I'm walking.

"We just have to tell the truth," Wyatt continues. "We aren't to blame."

I raise my hand up to block the light so I can see Axel as he speaks. "Or we could call in an anonymous tip."

"That could work." Jonah agrees.

I also agree. It would still be reported but we wouldn't have to deal with any of it. We could get back to our regular lives without facing the possibility of jail time.

Before I can say I agree, Wyatt responds. "How would that work?" he says. "We are still tied to all of this and they'll figure it out."

"We could..." Axel begins.

Wyatt cuts him off before he can finish. "We could do the right thing and call the cops. It'll only be worse for us if we don't."

"I don't care what we do," I say to them, even though I know it's a lie. "But I'm driving back to the house to find Misty."

Nathan told me she ran away and hid somewhere. If that's true, I'm going to find her. He better have not lied to me. If I find out they killed her, I'm gonna ... I have no idea what I'll do. I can't kill them. I'll probably just come back and kick their head in. Even though it will do nothing to them, at least, it will be some kind of revenge in my eyes.

I place my hand on the driver's side door handle when Axel stands beside me and says, "I'll drive. Hop in the back."

Without argument, I move to the side and reach for the backseat door handle.

In front of the car, stood in the lights, I see Jonah stop Wyatt from walking around to the other side. He whispers something and they both walk out of the light, to our side and stand behind Axel, watching me. What are they doing? Aren't they coming?

The inside light turns on as soon as I pull on the handle. I swing the door open, take my eyes off my three strange acting friends, and look inside the car.

A gasp escapes me.

On the floor, curled up behind the driver's seat, sits Misty. Clutched in her hands, she holds onto my grey beanie that I had left on the seat. She flinches as the door opens and looks up at me with scared, wide eyes that change and relax as she recognises the one who stares down at her. Tears stain her cheeks and shine in her eyes. "Dory?" she says in a whimper.

Chapter 29

I notice the rips in her white dress and the dirt that ruins the plain material, but the red splotches on her chest catches my attention more than anything.

Her long brown hair has become knotted and messy, looking like a bird attempted to make a nest on top of her head.

I glance to the side to look at Axel for answers. He knew she was here. How did she get here? Where did she come from?

I don't have to say a word for Axel to understand what I want to know. "She snuck in while the two psychos kept us trapped in the house."

I put it together in my mind. She escaped Nathan and Chris, and ran out of the house. While she hid, we arrived. When we were taken into the house, tied up, and beaten, she came out of her hiding place and jumped in Axel's car before he led the two brothers away.

I look back down at my scared little sister, still nestled between the seats.

"Are you okay?" I ask, softly.

She gives me a nod.

Staring at the blood on her dress, I ask, "Did they hurt you?"

She nods.

My heart races waiting for her answer.

"He pulled my arm and hurt it." She lets go of the beanie with one hand and holds out her arm to me.

"What about the blood?" I gesture to the front of her dress.

She looks down at it. "It's not mine," she says. "It's Nathan's. Chris cut Nathan's hand and then he grabbed me." Still looking down, she mumbles, "He told me you wouldn't come for me."

"He didn't know what he was talking about," I tell her.

She looks up at me, sadness glossing over her brown eyes. "I thought you wouldn't care."

A pang hits my heart. I had always felt that way about Mum. I know Mum will never care about me or Misty. Now, I had done the same thing to Misty. What kind of awful person am I?

"I'm so sorry I made you feel that way," I admit. "I may find you annoying sometimes, but you're my little sister. I will always care about you." That's the truth. I couldn't accept her unfailing love for our mother when she never received any care from her, and because of that I abandoned her and treated her the same way. I hate myself for it.

Misty gives me a pout and pulls herself up, holding my beanie in one hand. She steps forward and hesitates.

I open my arms to encourage her and she throws herself onto me. Burying her head in my neck, she breathes heavy. I feel her heart thumping faster than mine against my chest.

Gripping her tight, I lift her up and move back from the car.

"I can't get service here," Wyatt says. He holds his phone up, waving it around, staring at the illuminated screen.

Misty pulls back but stays sat on my hip.

"We can head back to the house," Axel suggests, sounding unenthusiastic, "and see if we can call from there."

"Yeah. Alright." Wyatt puts his phone away and walks around the car to the other side with Jonah.

I set Misty back down on the car floor and scoot in beside her as she takes the middle seat.

Under her feet, on the floor, her stuffed rabbit lies face down. I wonder how she didn't see it. She had to use my beanie to cling to for comfort instead.

I stare at the beanie in her hands as she glances up at me. Looking down and back up, she places it in my lap with a weak smile, and I take it and put it on, returning the smile.

Leaning forward, I pick up the rabbit and hand it to her. She takes it, resting it in her lap, staring at it's worn and bloodied face. "Where's Mum?" she asks, quietly.

"She's at home," I answer, my heart receiving a crack.

Axel pulls the car back, leaving the black car in front of us, and turns around to drive down the dirt road.

Knowing about Axel's driving, we all put on out seatbelts and I buckle Misty up while she stares at her favourite toy.

While we drive, Jonah winds his window down and a cool breeze fills the entire car. It relaxes me a little and has me wanting more. So, I find the button on the door and watch the glass slide down until the air hits my face.

"Did she know I was gone?" she asks over the whipping sound of the wind, keeping her stare locked on her rabbit.

I don't want to give her the answer. "Yes." Of course she knew. Did you see the state you left the house in?

The moonlight flickers through the tall trees as we speed down the bumpy and winding road. I can tell we're nearing the end of the forest area when the thickness of the trees start to die down.

"Did she care?" she asks, drawing my attention away from everything out the window.

I stare down at the small girl who refuses to take her eyes from the old toy in her hands.

A lump forms in my throat as I try to answer, stopping the word from coming out. I wish I didn't have to answer, but I can't stay silent.

I could lie, but she deserves to know the truth. And Mum doesn't deserve the lie that will make her look like a better parent. Besides, I'm sure Misty would be able to see through that lie no matter how attached she is to our mother.

"No," I answer.

She goes quiet again. Then, without warning, her rabbit flies past my head and out the window. I watch it land in the dirt and get left behind in the darkness before flicking my head back to look at Misty, quizzically.

"Why did you do that?"

"I don't want it anymore." Her eyes don't meet mine, but rather stay down at her hands in her lap, avoiding the stares from everyone around her.

"Why?"

"She doesn't care about me," she says. "I don't care about her."

Her fingers find the end of her dress and she fiddles with the material, keeping her head down.

For years I've wanted her to accept her mother's abandonment and let go of whatever affection she had for her, but now that she's done that, I want to bring it back for her. She looks so sad and tiny sat between Wyatt and I. So young and innocent. So broken.

Wanting to give her comfort, I pull the beanie off my head, and place it over top of her hands. She takes it and looks up at me, moisture in her eyes making them glisten.

Giving her a smile, I get a half smile back and she pulls it into her chest, hugging it tight.

From the corner of my eyes, I can see Wyatt smile, Jonah grinning as he pulls his head back around the chair to face the front again, and Axel glancing back in the rear-view mirror.

She rests her head on my arm, and I pull it away to let her fall against my side, wrapping my arm around her small shoulders.

Chapter 30

Arriving back at the house, Axel pulls the car to a stop and Wyatt manages to get a single bar of service, allowing him to make a call to the police.

While he talks to the person on the other end of the line, I hold my breath. I watch Axel and Jonah as he speaks. I'm sure they stop breathing too.

Axel's jaw tenses and he sucks in a deep breath when Wyatt says, "They were both stabbed...No. One of them stabbed the other, we stabbed the other one in self defence...He was going to kill us..."

Jonah, holding onto his injured arm, rests his head back and closes his eyes while we listen to the recount of everything that happened inside the house.

And when Wyatt tells the dispatcher, "Yeah, we'll wait here," I let out a low, deep groan.

I assume the dispatcher used his cell phone signal to track down our location because the only thing Wyatt said about out whereabouts is we that didn't know where we were.

He drops his phone from his ear and tells us what we already know, "We have to wait here for the police to arrive.

We wait for thirty minutes before the first police car pulls up beside ours. The second car arrives moments after that and they're soon followed by five more.

We get out of the car as soon as the first officer does, but we're told to stay where we are and wait for someone to talk to us.

Axel and Jonah stand beside the car, watching the police officers walk back and forth. Wyatt sits sideways in the front passenger seat with the door open, leaning forward to talk with Axel and Jonah. I sit in the back seat with Misty still leaning against me in the middle seat, clutching my beanie in both hands.

A few more cars and vans pull up and all the officers talk to each other for several minutes before we're finally questioned.

Nothing too in-depth at first. They just want to know where the bodies are located, how badly we're injured, if anybody else is around, what happened to any of the weapons, and if we needed anything before the paramedics arrived.

We answered their questions honestly and they tell us to stay put.

While we wait they give each of us a bottle of water. All of them are empty within seconds except Misty's. She barely drinks half and I eye it off for a few minutes before I can't take it any longer and I ask her if I can have some. She hands it over with a smile and a nod, and I give it back with a quarter of the water left.

By the time the two officers come to talk to us, Axel and Jonah have joined us in the car. Axel takes his place behind the wheel and Jonah sits beside Misty and I.

Our doors stay open, and despite the noise from all the officers, Misty lies with her head on my leg and her feet resting in Jonah's lap, light snores emanating from her parted mouth.

Just as I'm about to wake her, she jumps in her sleep, the nightmare waking her up instead. She complains, telling me she hadn't wanted to fall asleep but it just happened without her realising. I soothe her and help her out of the car with me and the other three.

Before the officers ask their first question, the woman officer takes Misty by the hand and leads her to sit on the stairs of the house to question her alone—probably in a more sensitive way.

The man officer stands in front of our group and begins his long line of questions.

We explain everything, leaving nothing out. The three of them can only explain the last half of what happened, I'm left to tell about what happened before I called them.

I tell them about Mum, and about the barman that told me where to find Nathan. As soon as I mention him, I wonder if I should have kept him out of it, but he's probably my best alibi. Mum won't help.

They question us about my car and I confess about the car chase and crash.

I relive every detail. Mention every moment of failure and success.

When the two ambulance vans arrive the officer informs us that we've provided enough information for now and we are to be checked over by the paramedics.

We're separated into two groups. Jonah and Wyatt are ushered into one ambulance, and Axel, Misty and I get head over to the second one.

While the paramedics treat us for our injuries, I watch the police walk back and forth from the house to each other. Talking. Pointing to us, the house, and the road. Passing around paperwork.

The medics finish with Axel pretty quickly. He has several cuts and scrapes, and by tomorrow he'll have mult ple bruises, but nothing too serious.

Misty has only a few sore spots that could develop into bruises.

I take the longest out of the three of us to be treated. They start with the worst of my injuries. The cut on my hip and the slice on my ankle.

The disinfectant stings like hell and I have to grit my teeth and grip the bed I'm sat on to stop from crying out.

Axel sits on the spare chair in the ambulance and Misty sits on his lap, staring at me with anxious eyes. He comforts her by stroking her arm, but she doesn't relax even after I reassure her I'm okay.

After that, they check the bruising on my ribs, stomach, and legs, before moving on to examine my head for any serious injuries I may not know about.

Finally, they clean and patch up the small cuts and scrapes scattered over my entire body.

Once the paramedics clear us to go, we climb out of the ambulance and make our way over to Jonah and Wyatt's ambulance.

Wyatt sits in the spare chair while a paramedic wraps Jonah's injured arm in a bandage. They're both chuckling about something but stop when we arrive to ask us how we are doing. We tell them we're good.

The paramedic puts Jonah's arm in a sling and lets them know they're good to go. They both step out the back of the ambulance.

Before we walk away, she reminds Jonah that if his arm worsens he should go straight to the hospital.

As we leave her to clean the mess of empty plastic packages and bloody gauze pads in the back of the ambulance, I ask about his arm.

"She did a couple of checks and said that it's probably not broken but the only way to be sure is to have it x-rayed," he explains. "I couldn't be bothered to go to the hospital so she just wrapped it and gave me some warnings."

"He's as bad as you," Wyatt says, looking at me, clearly remembering my previous refusal to go to the hospital.

After that, the police approach us again to let us know they already contacted my mum and the barman.

Mum refused to answer their questions and would hang up every time and eventually stopped picking up all together. That doesn't surprise me. They tell me they'll get in contact with her later, and I tell them not to hold their breaths.

The barman answered and was able to corroborate his part of the story. He's agreed to make an official statement tomorrow and he'll turn over the security footage that proves Nathan left with my mum and I was at the bar the next day.

One police officer talks to us, mentioning that next time we should call the police instead of risking our lives to deal with it alone. We all agree, saying next time we will, and Wyatt says, "Hopefully, there will be no next time."

I agree too. However, while I think about it, if I had one chance to go back to the beginning and call the police instead, I'm not sure I would take it.

After seeing Chris kill his own brother without remorse just so he could get to us, I don't doubt he would have killed Misty the second he heard the sirens or saw the cars. I believe I made the right choice. Or maybe it's just because I want to believe I chose right.

CHAPTER 31

S itting on the stairs of the house, we watch the police. Several scurrying about; searching for paper work, trying to find other officers, collecting evidence. Some stand around; talking to other officers, sharing papers, writing things down. Others do their own thing; searching the ground with torches, watching other officers work, talking on their two-way radios.

A couple officers walk in and out of the house, passing us without a word, carrying objects placed in see-through plastic evidence bags. The rope. Tape. The pieces of the soap dispenser I shattered against the bathroom wall. A white bloodstained rag. Multicoloured markers. And several more items I don't recognise or get a chance to see.

Misty clings to my arm, resting her head against me. She asks me for the hundredth time, "When can we leave?"

Each time, I have to tell her I don't know. An officer told us to stick around for a little longer in case they have anymore questions or need to know anything else. I swear it's been longer than a 'little longer' though.

We're all tired, sitting on the top stair of the house.

Jonah lies on his back with his legs draped down the stairs and his eyes closed, although I'm pretty sure he hasn't fallen asleep yet.

Next to him, sits Wyatt. He rests his in his hands and leans his elbows on his bent knees. I notice him taking long, slow blinks while he stares into the distance ahead of him.

I sit next to him, leaving a gap between us as a pathway for the officers. I stare at everything around me to keep my eyelids from drooping. Leaning back on one arm, the arm that hasn't been claimed by Misty. My aching legs sprawled out, down the stairs.

Axel leans against the railing post, facing the rest of us. He stretches his legs out in the space between Misty and him, resting his head back against the post. His distant stare remains trained on a spot above our heads, the same spot he found when we first sat down. He has the same sleepy blinks as Wyatt.

Misty refuses to sleep even though I've told her she can and I'll make sure she's safe. But no matter what I could do, it's this place that make her feel unsafe. I don't blame her.

It feels strange being this close to someone. I should have realised if I gave Misty my attention all these years, I would have received the affection I've craved for so long. I just had to care about her a little. Instead, I left her to be starved of warmth and love. I allowed her to suffer the way I always have.

I never appreciated her. I don't deserve her now. I don't deserve to have her holding onto me right now as if she'll lose everything if she lets go. She deserve the world. But right now, I'm all she has. So, I won't be selfish or push her feelings aside again. I'll do everything I can to make her happy and safe. Not for me. For her.

With all the time for my mind to wander, I think and worry about what will happen next. Where will Misty and I go? Will we have to go back and live with Mum until I can afford it? I hope not. After everything, the last thing I want to do to Misty is force her back into that house with that woman. I haven't asked her if she wants to go back or not, but after I saw her throw the stuffed rabbit out the window, I'm certain she finally hates her and wants to stay far away from her.

So, if that's the case, I can't go back home. But where will we go? How will we live? What can I do? I've never felt this useless before. I'm not ready for any of this.

I've spent years dreaming about moving out and living alone. I searched for houses and apartments to rent or buy, looked for jobs I could get into that would support me, and figured out how much money I would need to leave. But now, all of my gathered information is useless. All my research and figuring out is wasted and unusable.

I can't move into a space for one person. I'll need more money than I had estimated I would need to leave. I have to think about Misty, and put her education into consideration.

My head begins to pound and throb from the thousands of thoughts and questions whirling around in my head. The exhaustion doesn't help but rather makes my head ache and spin more. Deciding to clear my mind and worry about everything later, I close my eyes and let my head flop back, wishing I could fall back onto a bed.

Chapter 32

By the time the police approach us again, Wyatt had moved to lean against the wall of the house beside the front door. Axel rests back, almost lying down, his shoulders pushed against the post holding him up. Jonah snores lightly. I moved halfway down the stairs to lean again a railing post like Axel had done at the top.

I watch Misty sat on the bottom stairs, sorting and playing playing with flowers she picked from the garden beside the stairs.

She drifted off to sleep for less than a minute and jumped awake like she had done in the car. "I want to leave," she told me, her voice weak and soft.

"I know," I said, wanting the same thing. "Soon." I had no idea if I was lying to her or not, but I wanted to believe it as much as she needed to hear it.

She stood up, explaining that she didn't want to sleep here, and made her way to the bottom of the stairs. As she started picking the flowers from the ground, I warned her not to disappear from my sight, and after collecting a handful, she sat on the last step. Picking the petals off. Sorting them into several small bunches.

Wrapping and weaving their stems together. Anything to keep her distracted and awake.

Choosing the four best looking flowers, she handed them out to us. Axel took his and rested it on his knee. Wyatt held onto his for a while before he sat it down next to him. She placed Jonah's on top of his slinged arm and it hasn't moved since. And I still fiddle with mine between my fingers.

The fragile stem has split and bent. A single petal fell between my legs minutes ago.

She's counting the ones she has left when an officer walks over to us to tell us we can leave.

"Someone will be in contact with you later," he says, "if we need answers to anymore questions or we need you to update your statements, but for now you're good to go.

Axel stands and gives Jonah a small nudge on his good arm with his foot to wake him up. Opening his eyes and looking around, Axel tells him, "We can leave now."

Before the policeman walks away, I catch his attention and ask if we're in trouble or can expect any kind of punishment or consequence.

With a warm half smile, he reassures us that although there will be an investigation we shouldn't have a problem unless they find proof that we're lying or believe we had intent to kill.

He walks with us back to our car and explains the situation after letting us know that we can't talk about it with anyone.

After hearing all the information we've given them, everything seems to make sense and line up with everything they have suspected for months.

He tells us that they've been investigating Nathan and Chris for a while now for multiple crimes. Apparently, they are both suspected for multiple thefts and for fraud. Chris has been on their radar for a while, suspected for several beatings and even a couple of missing people and an unsolved murder of a man two years ago.

I can't help my slack jaw as I listen to him talk as if he's explaining a math equation.

With no evidence able to convict them, and no witnesses or victims coming forward to testify in court, they've never been able to catch them. They suspected they had a safe-house somewhere, but they were never able to locate it or prove it. So, the investigation always came to a stand-still.

They believe the forest where the two of them lie now, hold at least two missing people under the earth. A team will be brought out later to search for bodies and other pieces of evidence.

We're lucky to be alive, I hear him saying under his words. I believe it.

If everything they say is true, we were in a lot more danger than we thought. Nothing would have stopped him. We would have been his next victims he had to hide.

I don't have the tiniest bit of doubt that he was going to kill Misty. Whether we found him, the cops turned up, or he wasn't disturbed at all. Misty was going to be murdered.

"But you don't have to worry about any of that anymore," says the officer with the name 'Gidlow' on his shirt. "We'll deal with everything. Go home and get some sleep." He leaves us, walking towards a cop car and the officer that first questioned us.

We climb into Axel's car, taking the seats we have apparently assigned for ourselves. Misty rests her head back against the seat and closes her eyes. She holds my beanie she had left on the seat.

I tell her to buckle up, and she replies with, "Mm hm," but doesn't move. I reach over her and do it for her.

Axel navigates his way around the cop cars and the officers, and picks up speed when we reach the open dirt road.

With the bumpy movement, Misty falls to the side, resting her head on Wyatt's arm. He looks down, smiles, and lets her head fall onto his lap.

She's the reason we did this. She's the reason for our beatings and pain. But I know I would do it all again just to have her safe in the car with us.

For a quick moment, I imagine what it would have been like if Misty had died tonight. The overpowering sense of failure, heavy in the air. A paralysing emptiness filling me. I would stare at the vacant seat beside me, wishing she was there, wondering if I could have done something different for a different ending. Guilt suffocating me.

I glance down at Misty. Her dirty white dress reflecting the silver moonlight. She's there. She's safe. Alive. We saved her. Everything is okay right now.

I let my body flop around from the movement of the car, closing my eyes and enjoying the fresh air that rushes in through the open windows.

"Will you guys agree to go to the hospital now?" Wyatt asks over the wind.

"Nah," Jonah replies without looking back. "The paramedic said I didn't have to."

"Yeah, and mine said anything from the car crash wasn't life threatening," I say.

"Are you guys serious?" he replies. I can imagine the eye roll he gives us, unnoticed in the the dark.

"I just want to go to bed," Jonah answers. "Don't you?"

"Well, yeah," he mumbles, "but… um…but…" He trails off, unable to come up with an excuse.

"It's alright," I reassure with a smile he can't see. "We're fine."

Wyatt huffs out a short laugh. I see his silhouetted figure rest his head back against the seat and glance into the moon-lit landscape out his window.

Empty space. Rocks. Tall, dead grass. Uneven ground.

We pass my wretched car, and I can't take my eyes from it until it's out of my sight.

As we pull onto the smooth road, Axel says, "Where to now?"

Wyatt pulls his head away from the window. "I have to go back to Jonah's house so I can get my car before I can go home."

"Okay, and what about you, Dorian," Axel says. "Where are you going to go?"

With a quick think, I shrug my shoulders. Realising he can't see me, I say, "I don't know."

Oh but, I have endless possibilities. How could I possibly pick just one? My sarcastic thought makes me want to chuckle but I hold it in to not look like a lunatic to my friends.

"I can drop you home," offers Wyatt, uncertainty lacing his voice.

With that, Misty sits up, rubbing her eyes. Her long blonde hair flicking around her head from the wind. "I don't want to go home," she says in a soft, weak voice.

"Yeah," I agree, pulling her in closer to me. "I don't either."

Jonah spins around in his seat to look back at me through the faint silver light. "You can stay at my house if you want."

"Yeah. Sounds good," I say. Even if it's just for the night.

With a nod, he faces the front again, and says, "You can all stay if that would be easier."

"That might be better," Wyatt says.

"Yeah. Alright," Axel agrees. "We can try to get a couple minutes of sleep before the sun rises."

I chuckle.

CHAPTER 33

W hile we drive, with nothing out my window to distract me other than the shadows, my mind drifts once again, trying to piece everything together. Many questions arise, but I'm unable to any of fit them with answers, and I doubt I ever will.

It seemed like they trying to get rid of Misty's toys and things before they searched for her, but was there another reason for leaving her after she ran?

I wonder where Misty hid before we arrived. Would they have found her quickly?

How did she get away? Chris wouldn't have let her run, so she must have done something sneaky or brave.

What was her plan? Did she have one? Was her hope and optimism still shining bright, or was she expecting death and failure?

I know I will never get answers to some of these questions. Misty could answer a few but I can't ask her. I don't want to bring up this day to her ever. If she wants to talk, I will, but I can't force her to relive the worst day of her life. I won't.

A bump it the road knocks Misty's head down to my lap. With a deep sigh, she lifts her legs up onto the seat and Wyatt allows her to place her bare feet in his lap.

She stirs a couple times during the drive but by the time Axel pulls into Jonah's driveway, she's been in a deep, restful sleep for a while.

As slow as I can go, I move her off me, get out of the car. I worry about waking her, unsure as to how light of a sleeper she is, but she proves to be a very heavy sleeper when Jonah gets out of the car and without thinking, he slams the door shut. He receives a chorus of shushes and he quickly apologises but she stays sleeping, only moving to roll onto her back.

I lift her out of the car and carry her into the house, the pathway illuminated by the yellow lights streaming out the windows.

Cursing under his breath, Jonah tells us he rushed out without his house keys, and walks back to retrieve the spare key hidden under a rock in their garden. I follow Axel and Wyatt inside and Jonah waits to close the door behind me.

From the entryway, I step into the lounge-room to discover the remains of the interrupted hangout that I never made it to.

All kinds of junk food sits on the glass coffee table, some in white plastic bowls. Sour gummy worms. A purple can of Pringles. A box of Oreos. A small bowl of either skittles or M&Ms, I'm assuming skittles. Doritos, chocolate, sherbet sticks, gummy bears. Coca-cola, Sprite, Fanta. The empty packets thrown on the floor.

The TV screen shows a video game with the player's character on the floor in an awkward pose, and the words "You're Dead" written over top of it. The cordless controller lies upside down on the floor in front of the couch.

Wyatt walks over and switches the TV off. Axel starts to clean the food off of the long couch. Jonah gestures me to follow him, and he leads me through the house to the spare bedroom where I lay Misty down on top of the covers.

Before Jonah walks out, I ask, "Do you have a spare shirt I can put on her."

"Yeah," he says and walks out, returning moments later with two, letting me know I can wear the other if I want.

He walks back to help the other two clean up while I struggle to take Misty's dress off without waking her, throwing it on the floor, and battle to put Jonah's blue shirt on her. I then pull the covers out from under her, lay them over her, and place my beanie back in her hold.

Standing at the doorway, with my hand on the handle, waiting to pull it close, I stare at her. Watching her chest rise and fall. Her dark eyelashes fluttering above her cheekbones. The mess of hair that will need to be brushed tomorrow surrounding her head. In this moment, I'm so thankful to everyone and everything that happened tonight that allowed me to get her back.

I shut the door, leaving the dull light on, and meet up with the boys in the living room to help them finish the cleaning up. Picking up the rubbish and putting away the rest of the food.

Jonah disappears and returns with a folded brown blanket and a light purple pillow carried on his good arm. On top sits two shirts. He throws them onto the couch, and Wyatt and Axel accept the shirts,

"Anyone want a shower?" he asks.

We all agree to shower tomorrow. We're far too exhausted and with the new bandages, we don't want to worry about taking them off now, and having to replace them. So instead, Jonah gets us a washer each and we head into the kitchen and use a bit of water to wipe the dirt and grime from us.

Walking back into the living area, Jonah asks, "So, Dorian. You'll sleep in the bed with your sister, right?"

I give him a nod.

"And one of you two," he continues, gesturing to Wyatt and Axel, "can sleep on the couch, and the other can either sleep in my parent's room or in my bed with me."

"Couch!" Axel shouts. "Dibs!"

Wyatt looks at Jonah. "I am not sleeping in your parents bed."

"Why?" I tease. "You don't want to sleep where Jonah was created?" I crack a smile at his disgusted face and Axel laughs.

"So, my bed it is," Jonah says.

"I don't care." Wyatt holds his hands up. "Just not your parent's. Especially after the image Dorian just put in my head." He grimaces.

My smile grows.

As they walk away, Jonah flops his arm over Wyatt's shoulder and pulls him in close to him. "Great," he says. "We can snuggle and spoon."

Wyatt shoves him away, making him laugh, and says, "Not happening. You have a queen sized bed. Plenty of room to put between us."

They both look back to say goodnight.

Jonah stops and Wyatt waits up for him. "Help yourself to any food, and the spare pillows and blankets are in the cupboard in the hallway if you need any." He turns and keeps walking with Wyatt. "If you need anything, don't wake me."

Axel throws the pillow at the end of the couch. "See ya at four in the afternoon when we all wake up."

Everyone laughs and agrees.

Before Jonah and Wyatt disappear through the doorway, I catch their attention. "Hey."

They stop and turn to look at me, still smiling and laughing as Wyatt swats Jonah's hand off away from his as he tries to hold it.

"Thanks for everything you did tonight," I say with all serious-ness. "All of you. And sorry for dragging you into the nightmare and getting you all hurt."

"It's no problem, bro," Jonah replies. "Of course we'd help."

"Yeah," Wyatt agrees. "And you don't have to apologise. It's not your fault."

"Thanks," I say.

"We'd do it again, right guys?" Axel says looking back at them.

"Yep," Wyatt answers.

"Not even if you paid me." Jonah receives a slap to his upper arm from Wyatt and he laughs. "Definitely," he agrees.

"You guys are the best," I say, smiling.

"Don't get mushy." Jonah turns around and walks through the doorway. "Go to bed. Goodnight."

Wyatt follows him and before they get too far away, I hear Jonah say, "Shotgun being the small spoon." Wyatt groans, and Jonah laughs.

Axel turns to me. "You doing okay?"

"Yeah," I answer, but I don't know if that's the truth or not.

"You sure?" he says, looking unconvinced.

"Yeah," I say again. "I'll be better after I sleep for fifteen hours." That could also be a lie.

Axel chuckles and I turn to leave.

"Night, mate," he says.

"Night," I reply. I stop at the door and look back at Axel tossing up the blanket and letting it fall over the couch.

"Honestly," I say, taking his attention from the make-shift bed. "I can't thank you enough." The entire night flashes through in my mind at full speed, replying everything within a second. I have no idea what I would have done if they didn't come to my aid. "I owe you my life."

"You took a beating for me," he tells me with a smile. "We'll call it even."

I nod and smile. "Okay."

"We're here for you, mate," he continues. "No matter what. Now, go get some sleep."

With a short smile, I nod and leave him alone.

Walking into the spare room, I find Misty flipped over onto her stomach, tangled up in the blankets. Her arms stretch out to the side as if she's purposely trying to take up as much as the bed as possible. In one hand, my beanie.

I flick the switch on the wall beside the door and the room plunges into darkness. With help from the silver light filtering in through the windows, I make my way around the bed and climb in beside Misty, pushing her arm back to the middle of the bed.

Before I lie down, I pull my shirt over my head and toss it onto the floor. I can't be bothered to find Jonah's shirt he gave me, so I collapse onto the pillow and pull the blankets over me.

I shut my eyes and when I open them again the sun blinds me.

CHAPTER 34

The brilliant golden light fills the room. The trees blowing in the breeze outside the window create dancing shadows on the bed.

I squint and turn away from the blinding window to find the bed empty on the other side. Untangling the blankets off me and throwing them to the side, I sit up, groaning, tense with an aching pain.

My beanie sit on the edge of Misty's side of the bed, and I reach over and pull it on to hide my wild, tangled hair.

It takes me a moment to gather the strength and motivation I need to get of out the bed. My muscles protest the entire way up and I let out an extended groan.

Purple bruises cover my abdomen and chest. The cut on my hip, under a bandage, burns, and I wonder how I could have slept with the agony of it. I touch my fingers to my split lip, and feel the swollen area with my tongue.

Standing, my ankle protests with pain but I can manage to put weight on it without suffering too much.

Finding the red shirt Jonah had gotten for me on the floor, I throw it on while I walk out of the room and towards the kitchen, making a quick pit stop to the bathroom.

In the mirror, I check out my face. My lip feels worse than it looks. A little purple, a healing split, and noticeably swollen. I have a bruise below my eye and a dark bruise around my neck, and I notice a slight difficulty with breathing.

I hear the chatter and laughter before I step into the kitchen. A delicious smell wafts through the house, drawing me towards the room faster and causing my stomach to rumble.

Misty sits at the small rectangular table with Wyatt next to her at the end of the table and Axel and Jonah sitting opposite her. Plates, forks, knives, syrup, and a tall stack of pancakes fill the table.

I glance at the clock on the kitchen wall to discover the time. One pm. I expected to have slept longer. Maybe that's why I'm still not feeling one hundred percent. Although, I doubt sleep will solve that problem.

The blue shirt I put on Misty last night has been replaced with a purple and blue tie die shirt that I can imagine Misty picking from Jonah's cupboard herself. Her messy hair has been brushed, and the absence of the dirt that covered her skin last night lets me know she's had a shower.

I can see the scratches on Axel's arms. Bright red. But the bruise along his jaw stands out the most. Purple and blue. It looks sore, but he doesn't show it as he talks, laughs, and eats.

Wyatt's busted lip looks worse than mine. Cracked in two places. More swollen. Bruises cover his lips, nose, and cheeks. He holds onto his ribs.

Jonah's arm in a sling has a purple bruise peeking out from under the material. He has two small bruises on his face, but nothing like the rest of us. The way he sits and holds himself tells me he's suffering more in the abdomen and chest.

Misty bursts into another fit of laughter. I used to hate her laugh. I found it irritating, obnoxious, and too loud. But now, as it bounces off every wall, echoing throughout the house, I can't help but be grateful that I get to hear it again.

I'm sure I'll never hate it ever again after last night. Last night has changed so much. Myself included.

I have been closed off and withdrawn for years; hiding behind the towering, strong walls I built up when I was young. The frightful night has begun to break down my walls and open up my heart. It took one night to make me a new person.

I watch Misty throw her body back in laughter so much that I worry she may fall off the chair that she kneels on. Axel keeps talking to her, smiling, but over her laughter, I can't make out a word he says.

Wyatt and Jonah watch her, laughing along.

As she begins to calm down and settle back down in her seat, she notices me leaning against the doorway. "Dory!" she exclaims, sitting up on her knees again.

"Good morning, Miss sticky fingers," I say, glancing at her hand holding the piece of pancake, dripping with syrup down her arm.

She giggles.

I take the seat next to her and Jonah passes me a plate with a smile. He sits on the chair with one knee bent to have his foot on the seat.

Wyatt leans back on his chair, and Axel has begun stuffing his face with a half eaten pancake on his plate.

I take a pancake from the stack in the middle of the table and pour enough syrup to drown a small city on top of it. Without hesitation, I plunge my knife and fork into it and shove a large piece into my mouth.

I've never tasted anything so heavenly and flavoursome. My stomach can't wait, it grumbles once more before the food can reach it.

I begin shovelling in large amounts of pancake before I finish with the last mouthful. Within two minutes, I've devoured two large pancakes and reach for my third.

"What are you going to do now?" Axel asks me, finishing his plate off and reaching for another.

"I'm going to have to fast forward my plan and figure something out," I tell him, drowning my pancake in syrup and shoving a piece into my mouth. With a full mouth, I say, "We're not going back to live with Mum."

While going over the few options I have to choose from, my head gets sucked into a whirlwind. I slow my eating while I try to gain control over my racing mind. Not enough options. Too many problems. Too little solutions.

The ideal option would be a motel room, but how long will I be able to afford to stay there? I could find someone to rent with, but that could still take awhile and cost quite a bit.

To afford a place to stay, I need more money than I have saved back at Mum's house. To get more money, I need a better job. A better job will take me some time to find and even longer to get a job to accept me. To get a job to accept me that will pay me enough to survive with Misty, I need experience in that job. Experience that I don't have.

The idea turns my stomach and makes me feel faint, but I think the best option I have is to return to Mum's house and live with her until I can afford to leave with Misty.

I don't want to think about having to tell Misty that we have to return to the house she was taken from but I don't know what else I could do. Even if we stay at a motel, eventually, when I run out of money, we will have no other choice but to return.

I stop eating.

Jonah reaches forward and grabs another pancake. "You can stay here until you figure something out."

I'm ripped back into reality. His words have to repeat three times in my head before I can understand what he's said.

That's a lot to ask of him, I think. He's already done so much for me. "You sure?"

"Yeah," he says, attempting to cut the pancake with the side of his fork, having to use one hand. "My parents won't be back for another week and they won't care anyway."

I give it a moment of thought. Mum's or Jonah's? I don't think I need more thought on it than that.

"Alright," I say. "If it's okay with you."

"Of course. That way you don't have to go back to the..." He glances at Misty who eats her pancake with her hands like an animal. Syrup drips down her hands from the pancake in her grasp and down her chin from her full mouth. She seems oblivious to our conversation. "The witch's house," he continues, being more kid friendly than he would like.

I smile. "Thanks."

Chapter 35

We help clean up after breakfast and relocate to the lounge room where we find a channel on the TV for Misty to watch while we sit around talking.

"When do you plan on going to get all your stuff from your mum's house?" Wyatt asks me.

"I don't know," I say. "I would like to get everything as soon as possible, because knowing her, she would probably sell everything that's not hers, but I need to find somewhere to store it first."

"You could use our back shed," Jonah suggests.

I stare at him blankly.

"It's completely empty," he continues. "We've never used it. It's just sat there taking up space."

"Seriously?" Things can't be working out this well for me. How did I ever deserve these amazing friends?

"Yeah," he answers. "My dad has been thinking about tearing it down for months now because it's useless to us."

"Yeah, okay," I say, feeling a slight pang of guilt from accepting all the offers thrown my way, even though I know I don't have much of a choice. "But I can't do it alone," I continue, "and I won't do it while the witch is there."

Fear grips my heart at the thought of walking into the house and coming face to face with her one last time. I've always imagined the last big blowup I would have with her before I walked out the door. I felt I wouldn't be satisfied unless I could scream in her face what a terrible mother she is before I left. Now, I can't imagine anything worse.

I want nothing more to do with her. I never want to see her face again.

"We can go with you," Axel offers. "We can wait outside until she leaves so we know she won't be there and we'll leave before she gets back."

"We can't all go." I glance over at Misty, sat on the floor, eyes glued to the screen with some cartoon playing. "I don't want Misty to go back. Someone will have to stay behind."

"I will," Jonah says. "It's not like I would be much help." He nods down to his arm in a sling.

"Do you know anything about kids?" Wyatt asks him.

Jonah shrugs. "How hard can it be?"

"More difficult than if you had two working arms I imagine," Wyatt laughs.

"Nah, I could do it with no arms."

"Maybe you should stay and babysit Jonah," Axel says to Wyatt, and we all laugh at Jonah's exaggerated offended expression.

"It might be best if you both stay here," I say to Wyatt and Jonah. I look at Axel. "And you and I go."

Axel laughs. "Yeah, sure."

"The last time we split up, it didn't work so well." We all shake our heads and ignore the overjoyed Jonah chuckling on the end of the couch.

I turn back to Axel. "But one car might not be big enough if we're going to take it all in one trip." That's my plan. One trip and never go back.

"You can take my car too," Jonah says, smiling. "So long as you promise not to use it in a car chase."

"What's with you bringing up bad memories to use as jokes," Wyatt scolds with a smile.

Jonah shrugs and holds his head high. "It's better to joke about the past than to pretend it never happened."

"Wow. When did you start writing poetry?" I ask.

"Sometimes," he says, with all seriousness, "you have to be beaten and broken to discover what you're capable of."

We all stare at him.

"And I'm a expert bullshiter."

Later that day, as it nears the time I know Mum would usually leave, Axel and I get into the two cars and head over to the witch's house.

My heart begins to race when we arrive and I see her car still in the driveway. I pull into the driveway of the house opposite and Axel pulls in behind me.

I hope the owner of the house won't be back for a while.

While sitting here, waiting for her to leave, I panic by thinking she will realise I'm here and I'll be confronted by the last person I want to see.

I have to remind myself that I'm in a car she won't recognise, in a different driveway, and she's so self-centred that she probably wouldn't notice if a plane had crashed landed across the street from her.

Minutes pass, and I begin I think today might be the first day in years that she doesn't leave the house. She's probably taking advantage of the empty house she now owns.

I'll give it one more minute, I tell myself, and after that, if she hasn't left, I'll get out and tell Axel we'll come back another time, but that's when movement catches my attention.

Dressed in a skin tight and revoltingly short red dress, she makes her way to her car in her driveway. I have no idea how she walks in the towering orange heels without smashing her clown face onto the ground. And the amount of hairspray in her rat nest hair should be enough to topple her over, yet somehow, she stays upright long enough to get a miserable guy in her bed, or down enough drinks to give her a better excuse as to why she's on the floor other than a twisted ankle and a head full of rocks.

I lean the seat back and watch her by peering out as little of the window as possible, fearing that she'll look my way.

As soon as she's driven away and out of sight, Axel and I jump from our cars and run to the front door.

I use my keys to unlock the door and we enter to find the house the exact same way I left it.

"Holy shit," Axel exclaims, stepping into the dump.

"I know," I say, stepping over the coffee table.

Before anything, we search the house and take all the bags we can find. I steal a suitcase from Mum's room and two old ones from the junk-packed garage.

We make our way up to Misty's room but dump the bags in my room first. I know Misty owns multiple shiny and glittery bags, I'll use them for her stuff.

I find everything I thinks she would want and need. Toys she left behind when Nathan took her. Jewellery I find laying around. Axel helps me pack it all into bags.

I pack as many of her clothes I can fit into one bag, while Axel piles a another one full with colouring books, pencils, paints, makeup, and story books.

The hand-made art on her walls would go to waste here, so I take them off, place them inside a book about a superhero to keep them save and pack them into a bag. I leave behind the two pictures that Misty drew of Mum and the six that have the words, "For Mummy" written on the page. She doesn't need something to remember her.

We pick up her school books and pencil case off the floor, and I search around for homework, and anything else she might need for school; including shoes, socks, and her uniforms.

We carry the bags to the cars and on the last trip I decide to take the bedsheets and pillows and shove them in the back.

In my room, I pack the few belongings I own. Since I spent as little time in here as possible, my room holds minimal stuff.

I throw all my school books and text books into one bag, and fill another with my clothes.

Digging through my cupboard, I find the large jar filled with the money I stole from Mum and saved for this moment. While Axel runs bags to the car, I stare at it.

I can't believe the day has finally come. I thought I would have more warning or preparation. That I would be planning for it for days and months, and I would be counting down the hours until the day arrived.

I've thought about this day so many times. I've imagined about throwing the keys at Mum and telling her, "I want nothing more to do with you." Or having a moving van arrive and I start packing all my stuff up while ignoring her the entire time as she tries to argue with me and control me.

Instead, I'll be leaving without her knowing I was ever here. No grand exits. No satisfying ends. Just leaving. Walking out and never coming back. Nothing like I would have planned, yet somehow better.

Hearing Axel's footsteps running up the stairs, shove the jar in a bag and search for anything else I might need.

Just like Misty's room, the last thing I take are the bedsheets and pillows.

After that, we head to the bathroom to collect our toiletries.

On our last lap around the house, I search for any money Mum might have left lying around, and we take anything that might come in handy for when we find our own place.

A couple of plates, bowls, cups. A handful of cutlery. Towels. Her fancy liquid hand soap from her bathroom. Things we could buy on our own but I know it will make her angry and will let her know I was here. Just to annoy her one last time.

On the way out, I leave my keys on the counter, ready to leave this place behind me. As I place them down, something catches my eye. Tucked in behind a plastic bowl of junk against the pillar at the end of the counter, a pack of cigarettes.

I pull them out from their hiding space. Staring down at them in my hand, I think about the last packet I took. There weren't many left. I smoked the last one at the park. The pack that started all of this. The reason Mum left.

That moment feels ages away, a lifetime ago, even though it was only two days ago.

So much has happened. A lot has changed.

I tuck the box back in behind the bowl and walk out, locking the door behind me.

"How long until she realises, do you think?" Axel asks me.

"With her arrogance," I say, "Never."

Chapter 36

During the drive back, I sort through my thoughts and emotions, trying to figure out how I feel after everything.

My new found freedom gives me a sense of peace and excitement, yet at the same time, I'm filled with uncertainty, dread, and anxiety.

I worry that I might fail at this new life. A sweat covers my entire body. Stressing over everything, and imagining everything that could go wrong. My fingers wrap tight around the steering wheel until my knuckles turn white.

I'm so lost in my own head that I don't notice the car in front of me braking and pulling to a stop at the intersection until I'm right there. My foot slams down on the brake. I lurch forward. Thankfully, I avoid my second car crash in two days by only a hair width gap between us.

The car drives off as if nothing happened, turning around the corner and disappearing while I stay put, listening to my harsh breaths and my racing heart.

I can't do this. I've only ever had to look after myself. I've never had to worry about another person before. I'm going to fail Misty. Misty might have been better off with Mum. At least Mum could keep her alive.

A honk somewhere behind me pulls me back into reality and forces me to drive forward even though I haven't had time to collect myself.

No, I think as I pass through the intersection at a slow pace. Mum almost got her killed. It was because of Mum that Misty was kidnapped in the first place. But could I do any better?

For the rest of the drive, I stay out of my head. Anytime I notice myself drifting away with my thoughts, I pull myself back and focus on the road ahead.

Despite my anxious thoughts about the future, I'm in less of a panic in the drive back compared to the drive in. During the drive in, I had been frantic with worry, fearing a confrontation with my mother.

I'm sure that's the reason why the drive back to Jonah's seems shorter than the drive to my mother's. By the time I pull into Jonah's driveway, it feels as if I should have five more minutes left to drive.

Axel asks about the close call and the extended pause at the intersection the moment we get out of our cars. I tell him I was lost in thought. He accepts my answer and leaves it at that.

We leave everything in the cars and head inside to find Wyatt and Jonah sat on the couch and Misty jumping around in front of them. Misty rambles about something to do with fish and swimming while Jonah and Wyatt listen to her with smiles. The TV plays in the background on a low volume.

Jonah looks up as we walk in. "How'd it go?"

"Smooth," Axel tells him.

"We got everything," I say.

Axel grins. "And a little extra."

I smile at the idea of Mum returning home to find half her belongings missing, and knowing she won't do a thing about it.

I hope she finds my key first and thinks, "Thank God he's gone," before she notices I took half of the house.

"Is it all in the shed yet?" Jonah asks.

Axel and I say, "No," at the same time.

"Do you need help unpacking it all into the shed?" Wyatt asks, already getting to his feet.

"Yeah," I answer. "If we plan on finishing before the sun sets."

As Jonah stands up, Misty jumps towards us.

"You can stay here and watch TV if you'd like," I say to her as she stands at my side.

"I wanna help," she says, looking up at me with a smile.

"Alright then. Let's go."

As we walk outside, Misty skips ahead of the group, singing some kind of song that she makes up on the spot about getting her toys back and about today being the best day ever.

I swear Jonah enjoys it more that she does. He stumbles from laughing so hard.

We decide to start with Jonah's car but we end up opening up Axel's car and removing thing before we've finished half of Jonah's car.

Misty carries small things that she gets passed from someone to her and carries it to the shed where she passes it to someone else, that is until we reach her stuff and she gets distracted by everything. She ends up sitting on the ground beside the cars, surrounded by toys and playing with everything while we continue moving the rest.

The sun sets before we can store half of it and Jonah has to run inside and turn on the outside light so we can see to finish the job.

When we're done, I ask Misty to pick a few toys to keep out and we'll put the rest in the shed. It takes her a while to make two piles, constantly swapping toys back and forth. But she comes to a conclusion and she gladly places the others in a bag for the shed.

We all head back inside to watch some more TV, but when I announce a few of the doubts and internal struggles I'm having, the boys and I discuss the future, coming up with plans and figuring out solutions to possible problems.

When the time hits seven, and we realise no one plans on leaving any time soon, Jonah tells Axel and Wyatt they can stay as long as they like and they both decide to stay the night again.

Misty tells me she's hungry, and we call up and get three pizzas delivered.

That night, while Misty sleeps beside me, despite the encouragement from my mates and the problem solving they've done for me, I wonder how I'm going to screw this up.

How long will it take me to disappoint Misty? When will she realise I'm no better than Mum?

There's a reason why I was still living with the witch. I'm not ready for this. I'm far from ready, but I can't fail or Misty will suffer.

How will I make enough money to support us both? Where will we live? We can't stay in Jonah's spare room forever. Who knows how long his parents will put up with us.

How will I afford Misty's education? Will I have to drop out in my last year of school to allow her to finish primary school?

How can I do anything now that I don't own a car? What do I prioritise first, car or home?

What will I do if we end up living on the street?

We need food, electricity, water, transportation, living essentials, a place to live, clothes, insurances, and more. And for all that we need money that we don't have.

My eyes struggle to stay open, staring at the moonlit window. As exhaustion takes over, the questions and doubts move to the back of my mind, waiting patiently for tomorrow to arrive to terrorise me.

Before sleep consumes me, I think, How long will it take before Misty realises I'm not her hero.

Epilogue

One Year Later...

"Well, where did you take them off yesterday?" I shout, while spreading the peanut butter onto to the buttered white bread.

"I don't know," she yells back from her bedroom.

"How do you not know?" I place the sandwich in a container and pop it into her lunch box.

"I don't know."

"How does a person loose their shoes?" I place an apple in next to the sandwich and look through the fridge for any snacks I can give her.

At the other end of the small house, I listen to the doors opening and closing, hearing her moving things around in search for her school shoes.

"Found them!" she exclaims, running down the hallway to sit at the dining table to put them on.

After filling her lunch box, I close it up and go in search for her school bag that I find beside the couch. "Where did you find them?"

"In the bathtub," she tells me as if it's a normal thing. In this house it is.

"Why on Earth would they be in there?"

"I don't know."

I can't help but smile. "Hurry up and finish getting ready," I say. "You don't want to be late for school. And I don't want to be late for work."

Four months after that fateful night, I ran into the barman that had told me about the mechanic shop where I fcund had Chris.

"Hey," he said, recognising me. "You're the one that came to me asking about the guy who took your sister, right?"

"Yeah," I answered.

"Well, it's good to see you again, son. I was worried I might not get the chance to talk to you ever again." He pat me on the shoulder. "So, what happened? Is your sister alright?"

"Yeah," I replied. "She's good. I got her back with barely a scratch." On her, at least.

"That's fantastic," he smiled. "But I've heard some things that tell me it might not have been as easy as that."

I gave him the short version of everything that happened after I saw him last and by the time I had finished, he had his mouth hanging open.

"Shit, son!" he said. "How are you still standing here today?"

I laughed and told him, "By some miracle."

He laughed. "So, how are you doing now?"

"Surviving," I said, and explained our current situation.

We had lived in Jonah's house with him and his parents for two months before I found a place I could afford. His parents told me we were free to stay longer if I wanted but I already felt bad enough that I had stayed that long. They helped us move out and get on our feet and told me we were welcome back if we ever needed it.

At the time, we were living in a small, old apartment that barely fit the two of us, but I could afford the rent and that's what mattered.

It consisted of a tiny kitchen, a cramped bathroom, and one small bedroom that managed to fit one single-sized bed. I told Misty to take the bed and I would sleep on the floor beside her each night on an old thick blanket with a pillow.

Without a car, I had to walk her to her primary school, and walk myself to my high school and my work. Thankfully, both our schools were close to each other and were only a fifteen minute walk from our temporary home, and my job was a thirty minute walk. Fifteen if I left from school.

I had been on the look out for a cheap car but I couldn't afford the cheapest ones I could find, and the search for a better job that paid more always left me disappointed.

"Where are you working?" he asked.

"I work at 'Just Organic'."

"That tiny fruit and veg store across from McDonald's?"

"Yep." I had been stuck working at the same job I had gotten when I was thirteen, making almost not enough for two people to survive.

Everything I told him was just me answering his questions and venting to get it all off my chest. I never expected him to get involved or give me a solution, but in a single moment, he changed mine and Misty's life forever.

"I should have introduced myself before." He stretched out his hand to me. "Name's Dale."

It took me several seconds to piece it together in my head as I shook his hand.

Explaining he owns the bar, he offered me a job.

"I've been looking for a new server. Someone to tend the bar, and serve meals and drinks," he told me. "I was hoping to get someone with experience but I can make an exception if you'd like the job. It would definitely pay better than that small retail job."

I took his offer without hesitation.

I couldn't thank him enough in that moment. I'm sure I said thank-you at least ten times and I had to stop myself before he changed his mind.

I gave my two weeks notice to my boss at the fruit and veg store, and started working at the pub as soon as the two weeks had passed.

Dale gave me the training I needed and plenty of hours of work.

With the increase of income, I found a nicer place to live with rent I could afford. We moved in and I got to sleep in a bed for the first time in months.

A car became my next priority. One night, I had been searching through the cheapest cars but all of them looked as if they would crumble with a single touch, so I decided to higher the price on my search. After a minute, I came across a blue hatchback. It wasn't in bad condition and, best of all, I could afford it.

Thanks to Dale, I graduated. I had mentioned that I had been considering dropping out for a while so I could work more hours and he encouraged me to stay and finish, promising me full-time work if I graduated.

He allowed Misty to sit in the back during out-of-school hours so I could work more without worrying about leaving her home or finding someone to look after her until the end of my shift.

At the end of each night, he allowed me to take home any leftovers that were going to be thrown out. This meant, Misty and I got to enjoy proper meals for the first time in a long time. I swear, I will never eat two minute noodles again.

After I finished school, Dale held up his promise and allowed me to work full-time. More hours and more income, equalled a better life for the two of us.

I proved to Dale that I was reliable and responsible. In return, Dale trusted me completely and, with an understanding of my situation, he let me off the hook if I ever turned up late or had to leave early. He even allowed me to take days off if Misty ever needed me at home for any reason.

Because of him, I now have my license to handle and serve alcohol and he taught me some tricks and tips for mixing drinks.

I love my job. I'm good at it. I'm so glad I was given the opportunity. And I will be forever grateful to Dale, who has given me everything and more. A job. A decent-sized pay check. Education. Experience. My sister. And a reason to get up in the morning.

With my savings continuing to grow, we were able to move again. Into a place we could make a home. I made the place intimate and welcoming to give Misty a safe place that she will feel secure in.

To this day, Misty hasn't seen or spoken to Mum since the day she left her in the care of her kidnapper to buy a pack of cigarettes.

I've seen her once since. She came into Dale's Pub two days after I started working there. I never spoke to her. She never spotted me.

I pointed her out to Dale and he kicked her out. She walked out and she's never been back.

I thought Misty might have missed her or asked to see her after a couple of months of living with me, but she's never done anything like it. Never asked about her. Never even mentioned her.

Without her, our lives have been so much better.

I'm happier. More responsible. I've learnt so much and changed a lot about myself. The last cigarette I smoked was that day at the park before everything happened. It was easier to give them up and break the habit when I had Misty to focus on and take care of.

I make sure she never goes hungry. Always putting food on the table. I never ignore her. She's my top priority and I won't let her suffer. We've grown close; our bond has strengthened, and our relationship couldn't be better.

Axel, Wyatt, Jonah and I still hang out, only now, we have a fifth member of the group. Misty loves them all.

She gets along well with Wyatt's younger brother, Elijah. He's one year younger than her and they both go to the same school.

Wyatt brings him along to our hang outs when he can so they can spend time with each other.

It's nice to see Misty have a normal childhood and to know she never let that dreadful day ruin her happiness or innocence.

The police last contacted us three months ago to ask a few last questions and let me know that even though they were convinced of our innocence a year ago, they were able to prove it. The officer on the phone told me they would contact me if they needed anymore information, but I haven't got another call back yet.

During a moment at the police station, while I recorded another statement and answered more questions, an officer let me know they had gotten my mother to talk. It had taken them three weeks to to get her co-operate in the investigation.

She refused all the way until officers acquired a search warrant for her home and found multiple bottles of pills prescribed to several different people. They bargained with her and made a deal to drop any charges to do with the pills if she explained everything she knew about that night. She panicked and sang like a bird.

She told them how Misty was taken, and why she didn't believe herself to be responsible. When they asked her what she had done when she realised her child was missing, she had to tell them she did nothing.

I found out that while the four of us were taking beatings and preparing to die just to get Misty back, she had decided to go out drinking and ended up finding another guy to bring back to the empty house.

After they got all the information they needed, they held up their end of the deal and dropped the drug charges, but instead slapped her with a ten thousand dollar fine for neglect and emotional child abuse.

I couldn't stop the laugh that erupted from me when the officer told me.

Three months ago, I picked up the box of Misty's toys that had been collected from the crime scene. Remembering the way she picked through the things I took from Mum's home and threw away everything that tied memories of Mum to it, I sorted through the box while she was at school and tossed anything that would remind her of Mum, including the blood-covered pink rabbit she had thrown out the car window.

One month ago, I became Misty's legal guardian. When she found out, she danced around the house, singing some kind of song that she made up. From what I can remember it included her, me, happiness, rainbows, ducks, a castle, and more.

I will never forget my favourite line she sang.

"Everyone is happy. And I am happy too! I have the best big brother in the whole wide world.

I love Dory. He loves me! He is better than cats and glitter and ice cream."

It might not be the best lyrics ever written, it doesn't rhyme, and her melody was all over the place, but it's still the best song I've ever heard. That might just be because it was about me.

We will both remember that terrifying night as the worst night of our lives, but without it we wouldn't be where we are today. Our lives have never been better. I'm not suffering through my days, feeling miserable and worthless.

Misty became the beacon that lead me from the darkness. She showed me love and made me feel wanted and needed. I'm determined to make Misty feel the same way. She deserves it and I have a lot of catching up to do after the last seven years.

"Ready," she chirps, plopping herself off the chair onto the floor.

"Alright," I tell her, placing her lunchbox into her blue bag and zipping it up. "Come get your bag."

She skips over and pulls her school bag onto her back.

I drag my red bag off the counter, snatching up a banana at the last second before I walk towards the door, with Misty straggling behind me.

Opening the door, I wait for Misty, watching her run around collecting the activity pages she had to do for homework.

"Can we get ice-cream after school?" she asks as she looks under the couch for another page.

"Yeah, sure."

"And can we go back to the water park again on the weekend?"

"We'll see."

"The boys can come." She pops back up, sheets of paper in her grip and a grin on her face. "And Eli too."

"Okay." I chuckle. "I'll ask them."

She walks out the door. "I can't wait."

I shut the door behind me.